LAND OF THE LOST

Young drifter Hal Harper's welcome to the town of Senora is to look down the barrels of the law — little knowing that the outlaw Tate Talbot and his gang are the elected sheriff and deputies. Talbot, with a wanted poster on his head worth a fortune, decides to collect his own bounty by killing the innocent Harper and claiming the drifter is the outlaw known as Diamond Bob Casey. Harper escapes — but only into the Land of the Lost . . .

DEAN EDWARDS

LAND OF
THE LOST

Complete and Unabridged

LINFORD
Leicester

First published in Great Britain in 2009 by
Robert Hale Limited
London

First Linford Edition
published 2011
by arrangement with
Robert Hale Limited
London

British Library CIP Data

Edwards, Dean.
    Land of the lost. - -
    (Linford western library)
    1. Western stories.
    2. Large type books.
    I. Title II. Series
    823.9′2–dc22

    ISBN 978–1–44480–550–5

Published by
F. A. Thorpe (Publishing)
Anstey, Leicestershire

Set by Words & Graphics Ltd.
Anstey, Leicestershire
Printed and bound in Great Britain by
T. J. International Ltd., Padstow, Cornwall

This book is printed on acid-free paper

*Dedicated to the lovely
Charlotte Stranks*

Prologue

There was little else but sand, sage-brush and cactus on the land just south of Fort Myers. It had been deemed suitable for an Indian reservation by faceless people more than 1,000 miles away. In truth, there were other reservations even worse. Had it been intended for the more peaceful tribes it would have worked. But someone had not known that Apaches were not to be regarded as peaceful Indians. They were a proud nation who had seen their once vast kingdom taken from them and were expected to accept the theft as progress. The older Apaches did just that. They had lost their stomach for fighting. They had lost too many of their young braves. Now they were reduced to little better than livestock, to be kept within the confines of the reservation in the same way as farmers herded their cattle on the range. The promise of regular supplies of food might have convinced even the younger Apaches but corruption was rife in the dealings between the distant Eastern government and those who were meant to ration out the provisions.

Within a matter of only months the supplies started to arrive either late or not at all. The government had paid for the food and other basic provisions but the men in charge of distributing these to the Apaches could not resist the huge profits to be made by selling them on to settlers, or anyone else for that matter. It all boiled down to money and greed.

Soon the younger Apache braves with hot blood still in their veins started to talk about escaping from their enforced confinement.

So it was the night of 18 July.

The sun had gone down at around eight and a large moon hung over the vast wasteland of sand. Twenty of the young warriors who had already proved their manhood before being brought like mustangs to this desolate land gathered in an arranged meeting. They had already worked out what they were going to do. Now they had to make their plans reality.

Although not the oldest of the braves, one of them acted as though he had lived twice as long as he actually had. His was an old head on young shoulders. He had no equal with either a knife or a gun. Yet all their weapons had been taken from them when they had been herded into the barren land.

Nazimo knew that it was pointless simply escaping. For it to work they required rifles and ammunition to survive and fight off those who would be sent to bring them back.

Apaches were survivors.

They could also fight.

Since the first outsiders had encountered them they had become known as a nation which seemed to be able to fight better than almost all other North American tribes. Apaches had a ferocity like the land in which they lived. It was said that the Devil himself had created this place. For hundreds of miles in almost every direction it was as if the sun was as hot as Hell itself.

Little wonder that Apaches knew how to fight. It was defiance which had allowed them to survive at all. Few other men who ventured into their land managed the feat.

Nazimo led the nineteen braves away from the rest of the small settlement along the desert canyon. All they had was their courage to defend them. But they knew that the trading post and the fort beyond had plenty of rifles.

Both were situated at the mouth of the canyon.

The young men with paint on their faces and torsos led their ponies slowly towards the first of their objectives. Nazimo had been watching and listening to those who worked and traded in the trading-post building. He had sat motionless on the wooden boardwalk for over a week, absorbing every word, watching every transaction. None of those inside the long wooden building had any idea that this was one Apache who actually understood their language.

The moonlight was against them but Nazimo refused to allow it to change his well-conceived plans. The braves moved across the sand until they reached the very mouth of the canyon. A barbed-wire fence had been erected across the fifty feet of expanse between two rockfaces. It was always locked at night and two cavalrymen were meant to guard it.

Yet for months the confined Apaches had not even tried to escape. They had remained quietly in the place that had been designated to them. Nazimo had noticed that for the previous week the soldiers who were meant to be sentries had stayed inside the long wooden building instead. Through the open windows he had seen them and the men who worked at the trading post playing cards and drinking throughout the long cool nights.

Nazimo reached the barbed-wire gates first. A hefty brass padlock hung on a sturdy chain between the two gates. Yet for all the lock-and-chain's strength the fence itself was made of weathered lumber poles. The barbed wire was loosely tacked to the uprights.

Nazimo tossed his rope rein to one of his followers and then placed a hand on both sides of the lock and chain. As quietly as he could the Apache warrior pushed and pulled the tall fence gates. His strong hands gripped the poles as he moved further forward and then backward. He knew that the fence posts would eventually give.

He was right.

On the third push the gatepost in his left hand snapped like kindling. The heavy chain fell. Nazimo opened the gates, then signalled his followers.

They moved as all Apaches moved: silently and fast. Even the unshod ponies knew how to be as quiet as their masters. Nazimo waved half his braves to one side of the trading post. They held on to the reins of all the ponies as Nazimo himself led the others to the open window.

Cigar smoke drifted out into the evening air.

Nazimo knew that none of his braves was armed. They would have to enter swiftly through the window one after another and somehow manage to overcome the men inside. They would have to kill or be killed. Then, if they achieved their mission without any of the men or soldiers firing a weapon at them, they would have to steal as many rifles, guns and ammunition as they could. Nazimo knew that it was vital that no shots were fired if the fort was not to be alerted.

Faster than the blink of an eye Nazimo leapt through the window. His braves followed in quick succession. There were six men inside the large room: two soldiers and four trading-post employees. Each of them had a gun on his hip.

Nazimo and his braves attacked.

The soldiers were slower than the other four men. Maybe it was because their guns were in buttoned-down holsters. They both grabbed their rifles as the Indians leapt on them. Both men managed to squeeze their triggers before they were killed. The trading-post men were no gunfighters but they had guns. Two of them managed to draw and fire their guns before Nazimo and his braves overcame them.

The sound of necks being snapped echoed off the log walls.

The other pair attempted to flee into the night. They opened the door and ran out into the arms of the rest of Nazimo's men.

There was no mercy.

Just the sounds of death.

Nazimo knew that the men inside Fort Myers would have heard the shots and known what was happening. Like a seasoned military general he made his braves collect a rifle and gun each and as many boxes of ammunition as they could manage.

Within a mere five minutes the small band of young Apaches was thundering away from the place where they had been imprisoned.

They were five miles away by the time they heard a bugle sounding from the fortress.

Then they rode on.

1

A merciless sun refused to stop burning everything below its vicious fury. Even the air was boiling as its vapour swirled around above the seemingly endless ocean of sand. Few men had ever ridden into a land like this willingly. The bleached bones of creatures that had made that fatal mistake were scattered in the white sand as far as the eye could see. Wherever the rider was, it had to be as close to Satan's lair as it was possible to get without actually being dead.

Even seeing was becoming harder and harder for the lone rider who eased back on his reins and brought the exhausted horse beneath him to a gentle halt. Encrusted salt from the perpetual sweat had almost glued his eyes shut. He lifted his hat and ran fingers through his wet hair before using it as a shield against the blistering rays of the sun. If there was a way out of this unholy place, he couldn't see it.

The horseman dropped from his saddle and stood beside his faithful mount. Every sinew in his young body hurt as though a wagon had ploughed over him. He panted like a hound dog and desperately attempted to find breathable air as his burning lungs inflated his aching chest.

Was there a way out of this place?

The question haunted him.

He clung to the long reins with gloved hands, as though afraid of losing his only chance of escaping this place. Yet if his eyes had not been caked with dried salt and sand he would have seen that his mount was even less capable of fleeing than he was himself.

Lathered sweat covered the exhausted animal. It looked as though it had reached the end of its own long ride. Its head hung as its blood boiled inside the once proud body. It snorted at the hot ground even more loudly than its master's own pitiful panting.

For what seemed like an eternity the man just knelt and watched his own sweat rain down from his head. Even doing this simple thing was not without pain. Within minutes he could feel the heat of the white-hot sand as it burned through the knees of his pants' legs.

A myriad thoughts washed through the mind of the horseman as he tried to fight off the inevitable death he knew awaited him if he were to close his eyes. He was tired but refused to succumb to the sleep he knew he would never awaken from.

The heat from the sand eventually managed to penetrate his clouded thoughts and bring him back to where he knelt.

Using all his remaining energy, Hal Harper gripped his stirrup and pulled himself back up to his feet. He leaned unsteadily against his saddle. He kept one hand holding the reins and the other gripping the latigo. Harper wanted to fall down and sleep the sleep of the dead, but he knew that as long as he kept gripping the saddle he could resist that desire.

His eyes tried vainly to make out the scenery but they felt as though branding-irons had been plunged into their sockets. He raised his arm and wiped his face in an attempt to dry the constant sweat that flowed like a waterfall from the hatband over his burned features. Yet his sleeve was like the rest of his bleached trail gear. It was soaked with sweat.

He lifted the canteen and shook it.

There was no reply.

It, like his throat, was bone-dry.

He then recalled having given the last of his precious water to the horse before sunup. It had been a futile gesture that he now regretted.

Was this where it would end? Out here in a land he neither recognized nor understood? Was thirst going to finish him off after he had managed to avoid the bullets which had tried to kill him?

The man reached beneath the belly of the horse. There was no way the animal could take him any further. He loosened the cinch strap, dragged his saddlebags from behind the cantle and dropped them on to the sand. They, like the canteen, were now empty. He patted the horse's neck and started walking with the animal in tow.

His high-heeled boots were not designed for walking. They were meant to fit into stirrups and hold a rider firm. Yet he was walking through the soft sand.

He exhaled and saw the shadows flash across the white ground before him. Startled, Harper's hand went for the holstered gun on his right hip. Then he realized what had spooked him. Four black wide-winged vultures circled above him.

They knew how close their next meal was.

Instinct had alerted them to the fact that there were two big meals getting closer and closer to their demise. They only had to wait as the hot thermals kept them floating above the horse and its owner. They had time to wait. Plenty of time to wait for such substantial meals.

Harper sighed heavily.

His thoughts returned to how he had found himself in this perilous place. He realized that if he had not run away from the guns which had tried to end his existence, he would not be in this unknown land. He would already be dead. Dead from lead poisoning.

Yet would that be any worse than this?

He was angry. If he had just taken the time to ensure his canteen was filled he might not be walking alongside a dying horse. But there had not been any time to do anything except flee the guns.

Harper staggered and heard the horse behind him do the same. Neither found the soft sand to their liking.

Harper could use his gun as well as if not better than most along the unmarked border, but he had never chosen to fight if there were an alternative. Now he doubted whether that had been wise. He should have killed all those who had tried to kill him.

But that had never been his way.

He tried to swallow but there was no spittle left to wet his throat. The dunes of sand rose in all directions like mysterious yellow mountains: mountains that seemed to move as if they actually were alive.

All the man could do was walk beneath them in the hope that their shadows would ease his and his horse's pain.

For nearly two days he had ridden.

For nearly two days they had chased him.

With every stride Harper asked himself the same question. Why had those men back in Senora opened up on him? He had barely been in the town thirty minutes when they had sought him out in the small cantina.

Somehow he had managed to escape their bullets. He had managed to leap through a window, find his horse, and then he had spurred.

But they had chased him.

Like hounds on the scent of a racoon they just refused to quit.

They chased him further and further south until the grass had ended and even the sagebrush no longer grew. Chased him into the endless dunes of sand and kept on coming.

Harper gave a sigh and led the slow horse up the side of a dune in an attempt to find a vantage point from where he might have a clue as to which direction to take.

But tired legs, both human and animal, were not designed to walk up hills of dry sand that gave way with every step. Somehow he managed to reach the top of the dune. He carefully patted his mount on the neck and screwed up his burning eyes once more.

It was hard to see anything through the thick haze of burning air. The dunes

17

rolled on for miles but there did seem to be something just before the horizon. The shimmering heat played tricks with Harper as he clung to his reins. It looked as though there was water out there!

Blue, inviting water.

Could there be a lake at the end of this torture? Again he tried to swallow.

Again he failed.

Could there really be water out there?

The question tormented Harper as he surveyed the rest of the land that encompassed him and his horse. Then as his unsteady legs turned him to look back over the sand he had already travelled across he felt his heart quicken.

Even the hot air could not conceal them from his burning eyes.

Five figures appeared, almost black against the arid landscape they were riding in. Harper rubbed his eyes again and focused for all he was worth at the riders, who seemed to vanish with every other beat of his pounding heart. The treacherous heat haze mocked him.

They were still chasing after him!

Or were they?

He gasped, steadied himself against the exhausted horse and gritted his teeth. It seemed impossible that anyone should keep hunting another soul through a land like this.

Were they insane? No sane man would ride into a land like this, he told himself.

Again he rubbed his eyes. Was it real or just another of the mirages that had tantalized him for the previous two days in this strange country?

Then Harper felt the heat of something pass within inches of him. The horse shied and instantly he knew what it had been. The sound of the gunfire echoed around him.

It was real.

They were still hunting him.

2

It had all begun two days earlier and forty miles north in a border town called Senora. Senora was by its very nature a dangerous place. So far away from the rest of civilized Texas, which was trying to rebuild itself after the war, Senora had become just another of those places where the law barely hung on to its tin stars long enough to find out the name of the men wearing them. The reality was that it was a town where outlaws and bandits found safe refuge knowing that the local sheriff would not do anything except keep his head down.

For the three months since the elections Tate Talbot had been sheriff of Senora. Unlike most of his predecessors Talbot had never been on the honest side of the law. It was also a fact that, until standing for office, Talbot had been known by many other names and was wanted dead or alive for each of them.

Tate Talbot sounded honest enough though.

Even if most of the townsfolk knew the truth they were not loco enough to mention it. For all of his thirty-nine years he had ridden along both sides of the long unmarked border between Texas and Mexico, using his skill at killing and rustling to make him wealthy beyond the dreams of most men. Becoming a sheriff had been his latest ploy to cash in on all the saloons, whorehouses and gambling halls within the sprawling, sun-bleached town's boundaries.

It had worked well and paid him handsomely.

In twelve weeks Talbot had managed to cream off ten per cent of every business in Senora. His personal wealth now accounted for more than half the money in the town's only bank.

Even the rest of the outlaws who

used Senora as a place to rest their bones between rustling cattle knew that Tate Talbot was a man they could trust not to interfere with them as long as they gave him a cut of their profits.

Yet even Talbot could not resist the mouth-watering wanted posters that were sent to him once a month by stage. Most were for such paltry sums that it was not worth his while even considering trying to collect the bounties, but there were a few that just could not be ignored.

It was as tempting as honey to a hungry bear but the wily Talbot knew that he could not turn on the outlaws who filled the saloons and brothels and spent their ill-gotten gains in Senora without risking their retribution. If he were to collect reward money safely he had to figure a way of doing it while also keeping the free-spending drifters sweet.

But he kept looking at the wanted posters. He kept trying to think of a way in which he might be able to make that one big play that would enable him to be so rich that he could buy himself respectability far to the west, in a city like San Francisco. It was OK being rich in Senora but it meant nothing to a man who had always wanted more. To be rich in a city on the Californian coastline was a different matter. There his money could buy things which simply did not exist in this dust-weary town.

All Talbot had needed was that one wanted poster with a reward so large it would be worth the risk of incurring the wrath of the outlaws and bandits.

He knew that it would arrive one day. One day he would hold in his hands the key that could unlock him from the life he found himself living.

It had been close to sundown when the noon stage had eventually drawn into town. Talbot, a well-built man, had walked the fifty or so yards from his office to the stage depot and watched as the mail bag was thrown down by the shotgun guard to the depot clerk.

'Anythin' for me, Luke?' Talbot had asked the guard who was climbing over the various bags on the top of the coach.

The bearded man paused and looked down at the boardwalk where Talbot was standing with thumbs tucked into his gunbelt.

'Yep. I seen them put a whole heap of wanted posters in the mail bag for ya, Sheriff,' the guard said through a mouthful of broken teeth. 'Git Clem to give 'em to ya.'

Talbot nodded, turned and slowly trailed the clerk into the depot office. He rested his hands on the top of the desk and watched the clerk with eyes that had seen more than most in their time. Sunlight was low and its dying rays danced across the office wall.

'I'll have them posters, Clem,' Talbot said in a deep drawl.

The clerk opened up the bag and searched through the mail until he found the posters, tied together by blue string. He handed them to the lawman and tilted his head so he could see from under his black visor.

'Ya sure likes them posters, Tate,' he commented.

Talbot grinned. 'Yep. One day I'm gonna find me one with big money printed on it. Wanted dead or alive!'

'Ya itchin' to kill some critter, Sheriff?'

'Damn right!' Talbot smiled. 'I ain't killed nobody in a month of Sundays. A man can get rusty.'

The clerk gestured at the window, then struck a match and touched the wick of the candle on his desk. As the flame lit up the office the small man blew the match and tossed it out into the street.

'The town's full of outlaws, Tate. Ya could go kill some of them and make a few bucks. I reckon if ya just closed ya eyes and fired down the street you'd hit at least one varmint wanted for something.'

Talbot nodded. 'But most of them varmints are my pals, Clem. Besides, they ain't worth a new saddle between 'em. Ain't worth my while wasting lead on them.'

The clerk busied himself as the lawman walked out into the fading light and strolled back to his own office with the posters tucked under his left arm. The words had been true. Most of the outlaws and bandits who roamed freely in town were dangerous killers without an ounce of morality between them, yet for Talbot to go up against any of them would be suicidal for a man so close to the other side of the law. Talbot knew that if he were to try to claim the reward on anyone, it would have to be someone neither he nor any of the other trail trash in Senora had ever encountered. The bounty would also have to be in the thousands of dollars for him even to bother.

Upon arriving back in his office, Talbot had lit the lantern on his desk, turned up its brass wheel and sat down. He broke the string and placed the pile of posters before him. It was like looking at a potential meal. His mouth started to water in anticipation.

One after another he studied them, turning each one face down as he got to the next.

As always there were vague descriptions of the outlaws who seemed to have more names than any honest soul. Some had even more names than Talbot himself. Heights varied, as well as hair colouring. Few of the posters had any truly accurate information and none could even agree on the outlaws' ages. *Thought to be between twenty and forty* was printed on at least half of them. Only a few had crude photographic images which could have fitted nearly anyone in town. One poster after another turned into one disappointment after another.

Then as Talbot had almost reached the last poster his hand stopped turning and he drew the stiff paper closer to him. He turned the wheel of the lantern up once again. The office became brighter. This was the one poster he had never even imagined was in circulation.

It was the amount that had attracted his full attention first.

'Twenty thousand dollars, dead or alive!' Talbot muttered aloud.

A crooked smile etched itself on his face as he looked at the poster in his left hand. 'Diamond Bob Casey.'

He shook his head and laughed out loud. It was a joke only he understood. It was perfect. Diamond Bob Casey was wanted dead or alive for $20,000.

Tate Talbot rose from his chair with the poster clutched in his hand. He looked out of the window of the office as the street lights were being lit by a small man with a long pole and a flaming rag at its end.

He kept laughing.

Not one of the other wanted men in Senora knew why their sheriff was so amused. If they had they might have started shooting in his direction.

For, ten years earlier, Tate Talbot himself had used the name of Diamond Bob Casey. The lawman pulled a cigar from his vest pocket and placed it between his teeth. He leaned over the glass funnel of the lamp on his desk, lit the tip of the cigar in the flame, and sucked in the smoke. It filled his lungs as his mind raced. Of all the wanted outlaws in Texas and beyond, it was he himself who was the most valuable.

He inhaled the cigar smoke deeply. But how could he get his hands on the money someone had placed upon his own head? The question burned into his mind.

Then, as if by divine providence, Tate Talbot was given the answer he had searched for.

As smoke drifted from between his teeth the man with the tin star pinned to his shirt saw the lone rider pass the window of his office. It was a man whom he did not recognize but that made it even better.

A stranger.

A drifter.

A drifter who was doomed to become the dead body of Diamond Bob Casey.

29

All Sheriff Talbot needed to claim the bounty on his own head was a body. Any body would do. He still had the savvy that had served him well when he had been Diamond Bob, and he knew that he could salt the corpse with personal items that would allow him to kill, prove his case, and make his claim for the $20,000.

Hal Harper aimed his mount at the nearest cantina. He had no idea that, in the mind of the lawman who watched him from the sheriff's office, his fate was already sealed.

Sealed by a ruthless man who was going to do the impossible.

A man who was going to claim the reward money on his own head.

Talbot carefully folded the wanted poster up and pushed it into his shirt.

'Like taking candy from a baby,' he muttered. 'A lotta candy.'

3

As another three rifle bullets kicked up clouds of sand and buried themselves at his feet, Hal Harper somehow found renewed vigour. Without a second's hesitation he turned and leapt down the sandy slope, dragging the horse behind him. Both man and beast toppled head over heels and rolled downward as the unstable white granules beneath their feet gave way. It was Harper who reached the level ground first, but he was soon followed by his horse. Every last breath was knocked from the animal as it landed hard beside its master.

It was a shaken Harper who staggered back to his feet, dusted himself off and moved to the motionless animal. For a few moments the young man wondered whether his mount was still alive. He then saw the creature's long legs kick out as its startled eyes followed his every movement.

Reaching down, Harper grabbed hold of the loose reins and was about to tug at them when he heard something to his left.

Something that startled him.

The youngster spun on his heels and swiftly drew his Colt from its holster. He cocked its hammer and screwed up his sun-burned features in a vain attempt to see what had alerted his senses.

There was nothing to see. Nothing to focus upon.

Only another mountain of yellow sand looming amid so many identical others. Gun in hand, Harper turned full circle as if perhaps the noise had come from somewhere else. Somewhere he had yet to identify. Nervously he returned to the horse who was lying on its side with its saddle almost torn free. Harper checked the cinch strap. It was still intact. He told himself that he would be able to use the saddle again, if the horse survived.

'Get up!' Harper urged the winded animal as his eyes vainly searched every square yard of sand within view for a hint of what or who had made the disconcerting sound. 'Get up, boy!'

Then another bewildering noise drew his eyes and his gun barrel back to the dune. Yet he still could not make out what it was that was making the noises beyond the mountain of sand. Was it an animal, or perhaps something made by the hands of man? He could not fathom the brief tormenting noise, which did not linger long enough for his tired brain to work out the riddle.

He looked back down at the horse.

For three long years this animal had obeyed every command Harper had uttered. Never once had it refused to comply with its master's demands. Now it lay wide-eyed and pitiful at his feet.

The young Harper moved around the horse and checked that it had no broken bones. When satisfied he returned to its head and grabbed hold of the reins close to the metal bit.

'Get up! I'm in worse fettle than you are, boy.' Harper dragged at the bit until the horse eventually started to move its long legs and claw with its hoofs at the soft sand. It took a few attempts but eventually it managed to roll over and stand upright. Harper pushed the saddle back up on to his mount's high shoulders.

'Good boy!' Harper ran his left hand along the animal's neck. 'Good boy! Now come on before them backshooters behind us catch up and make glue out of the pair of us.'

As if the horse understood the words, it began to trot at the side of its master. The fatigued mount trailed Harper who somehow managed to ignore his own weariness and crippling thirst and actually run.

They had almost reached the nearest dune when they both heard the uncanny sound again. Both stopped in their tracks and looked in the direction from where they were convinced the strange sound had emanated.

'Whatever that is I got me a feeling it ain't gonna be good news for us, fella.' Harper held on to the reins with his left hand whilst keeping the gun in his right trained on the sandy prominence before them. They began to walk again, this time with more caution than previously. With each stride the horse kept turning its head and looking to where they had both heard the sound.

It too was frightened.

'You hear it as well,' the youth whispered. 'Thank God I ain't imagining it! I saw you look the same as me. There is something ahead over that damn dune. Something that's making them strange noises.'

For another ten minutes the man and his horse staggered and walked. Neither seemed to notice the blazing sun which continued to beat down upon them. The sand which covered their sweat-soaked hides gave them a little protection.

Their dazed minds were now upon

something besides their own pain. Something which might be more dangerous than the five riders who trailed them or the unyielding sun in the cloudless blue heavens that tormented them.

The horse was nervous because it, like its master, was slowly losing its battle for life against the unbearable heat and the lack of water. Only determination kept them upright and fighting the elements.

Neither was ready to die just yet.

With every step that Harper took he tried to recall the direction in which he had seen the image of the lake of blue water. He prayed that the lake might be real and not just another trick of the desert. He knew where the sun had been in the cloudless sky when he had been atop the high dune, and he tried to remain on course as he staggered through the hot dry land.

'We gotta keep heading thataway, boy,' Harper said to the animal as though it understood. 'That's where the lake is. We have to keep heading that-away.'

Suddenly another sound shook the air. This one was louder than those which had confused him. It echoed all around the man and his horse.

The horse reared up and kicked out at the very air itself as its owner hung on to the reins. There was no mystery in this particular sound though. This was a noise they both recognized all too well.

Rifles were being fired.

The only difference was that this time the bullets were not being aimed at them. This time there was another target.

The horse battled with its owner. Harper holstered his gun and pushed his gloved fingers into both sides of the bridle of the frightened horse until his hands were jammed there. Another shot rang out behind them. The horse tried to rear up again but could not lift its forelegs off the sand with the weight of its master hanging on to its head and neck.

'Easy, boy!' Harper shouted into the horse's face as it attempted to shake him free. 'Steady! You'll kill yourself if you get too excited!'

The tired animal slowed and then stopped bucking. It was too weary to fight the one man who had always taken care of it. Hal Harper held the head of the animal in check and stared off behind them at the largest of the dunes.

He could not see any of the five men who hunted them.

They had yet to reach the top of the high dune. Again shots rang out in the hot afternoon air. This time the horseman saw the lines of the hot lead as they cut up into the sky from beyond the mountain of sand.

He also saw two of the four circling vultures fall from the sky and disappear from view.

Harper sighed with relief. He pulled his gloved hands free and steadied the animal with soothing strokes across its lathered-up head.

'Easy, boy!' Harper panted heavily. 'I reckon we got ourselves some time. Them varmints must be hungry and they just shot themselves some dinner. Vultures must take a lot of cooking before you can eat the damn things.'

The exhausted man began to move again, with haste, away from where the shots had sounded. The animal kept pace with him as they found themselves ascending a slight rise between two towering dunes.

Again Harper paused. His eyes squinted from beneath the wide brim of his hat. 'I figure that we have to go another few miles in that direction, boy. Then we'll have all the water we can drink.'

Slowly Harper staggered down the rise. Cramp was beginning to gnaw into his leg muscles but he knew that he could not stop. He had to ignore his pain and keep going. Only death could stop the sweat-soaked man now. But there were five hardened riders somewhere over the highest of the dunes behind him who would be more than willing to dish out death given the slightest chance, or a clean target to aim at.

The further they walked the hotter it grew. It was unbearable. The very air around the man and horse was thickening like a fog. Yet no fog was like this, Harper thought to himself.

Then they heard the strange noise again.

Harper drew and raised his gun. He aimed to his right, into the swirling heat haze.

'Who are you?' he called out.

There was no reply.

Then he heard the sound once more.

Trails of sweat ran from his hatband over his forehead and into his eyes. Salt stung like a thousand hornets. Harper shook his head and tried to see. He wondered how much of his body's sweat he had left to lose.

He swayed on his feet, holding his gun at hip level.

'What the hell was that?' he asked

himself fearfully. 'That ain't no human making that ruckus.'

He blinked hard but the sweat kept stinging his eyes. They seemed to be on fire just like the rest of him beneath the remorseless rays of the sun.

'What is that ruckus?' Harper again asked aloud. 'Damn it all! I know that sound. What is it?'

He knew that he had heard it many times before but now his brain refused to tell him what he was listening to. He knew that if he were not so damned exhausted he would have already worked this puzzle out. But in the searing air through which he tried to see, his brain was filling with overheated blood. Blood that was cooking his very reason.

He gulped.

There was only one way to find the answer.

Reluctantly, Hal Harper led his horse on through the heat haze and towards the place where he knew the sound was coming from.

He had never been quite so scared in all of his short life.

But he kept walking defiantly.

If it were to end now, at least it would be on his terms.

4

Tate Talbot had not taken long to work out a plan, a plan which, he knew, would more than double his personal wealth overnight in one single swift and bloodthirsty action. He had waited for Hal Harper to dismount from his horse and enter the cantina before hurriedly leaving his office and walking along the long busy street to the Broken Branch saloon. With each step the lawman could feel his plan becoming a reality.

Even though it was only minutes since the desert sun had set, the popular drinking hole was full to overflowing. Sombreros made up a third of the hats which nodded at the bar and over the green baize poker-tables. Bargirls plied their trade in and around the tables with keen eyes on the men with the biggest stacks of chips before them.

Few heads turned as the man with the star pinned to his shirt pushed his way through the swing doors and crossed the sawdust-covered floor towards a door marked PRIVATE. Since taking office as sheriff Talbot had leased the small room in the Broken Branch so that his gang could do their drinking in private. Men like those with whom he had ridden for so many years had short fuses and fast guns.

There was no way that the man once known as Diamond Bob Casey wanted his men to ruffle the feathers of those who now found themselves paying him a percentage. Only when the saloon and whorehouses failed to pay their dues did Talbot unleash his gang upon them.

But keeping four men like them fenced in had proved harder than he had expected. They wanted to quit Senora and get back to their old ways. Get back to the open ranges where they could rustle prime beef on the hoof and drive it north to the plentiful supply of buyers. Buyers who never asked any questions.

Upon reaching the door Talbot turned the handle and entered the small smoke-filled room abruptly. He nodded at the four outlaws around the wet-topped circular table.

Will Henry, Frank Smith and the Davis brothers Liam and Ken all sat with cigars in their mouths and glasses full of whiskey in their hands. Two empty bottles remained beside an ashtray so full it could no longer be seen beneath the cigar butts and ashes.

'Tate!' Henry acknowledged the sheriff with a touch of his hat-brim.

The others looked up as Talbot dragged a hardback chair from the wall and sat down at the table.

'Boys,' Talbot said as he chewed on the remnant of his cigar and pushed his hat off his temple. 'I was hoping that you'd all be here.'

'What does our prim and proper Mr Talbot want?' Smith asked coldly. 'I thought you had forgotten all about ya old gang. We thought ya was out with them fancy friends of yours drinking tea and suchlike.'

Both Davis boys chuckled at the same time.

Talbot grinned. His eyes darted across the four faces as he silently reinforced his authority over the men who for the previous four years had been his gang.

'I got a job for you,' Talbot said.

Henry looked interested. He eased himself towards the man he had followed blindly in the latter part of his career as a rustler. The outlaw rested both elbows on the wet surface of the table and stared at the sheriff.

'OK! I'll bite! What kinda job ya talking about, Tate?' he asked. 'Rustlin' or bank hold-up? My gun finger is darn twitching for some action.'

'Neither,' Talbot replied.

'Neither?' Smith downed his whiskey, poured himself another three fingers and stared at the man he felt had deserted them by becoming a lawman.

'Then it must be a killin' ya want us to do. Right?'

Talbot smiled. 'I just want you boys to back up my play.'

Liam Davis looked at the sheriff. 'What kinda money we talking about, Tate?'

'A hundred bucks apiece,' Talbot told them. 'For maybe ten minutes' work.'

'I'm game,' Liam Davis said, nodding.

Smith pulled his chair closer to the lawman. 'A hundred bucks? Who we gotta help ya kill, Tate? The mayor?'

'Nope. A varmint called Diamond Bob Casey,' Talbot replied. He raised his eyebrows. 'Ever heard of him?'

Will Henry scratched his whiskered jaw. 'That handle rings a bell. He from up north?'

Talbot diverted his eyes from his top gun. 'I ain't too sure, Will. But I want him dead.'

Smith got to his feet. Cigar in mouth, he paced around the table and the four seated men as he sipped at his liquor. 'What's wrong, Frank?' Ken Davis asked.

'Now that's a damn good question,

Ken.' Smith paused behind Talbot. He rested a hand on the back of the chair and looked at his fellow outlaws. 'Something's sure wrong but I can't quite figure out what.'

'Tate's offering a hundred bucks to back up his play,' Henry observed. 'What's wrong with that?'

Smith continued on his way until he reached his own chair again. He raised his right boot and placed it on the seat. His eyes burned across the table at Talbot.

'Something's gnawing at my craw, Tate. I figure ya ain't telling us the whole truth about this job. Why would ya give us a hundred bucks apiece to back up ya play? What's in it for you?'

Talbot grabbed hold of the bottle and took a long swallow of the whiskey before placing it back down.

'Don't you trust me, Frank?'

Smith smiled wide.

'I never have trusted you, Tate. Ya devious. Like a damn sidewinder. Devious.'

'Fair enough.' Talbot spat his cigar at the floor and rose back to his feet. He stared at Smith and then took two steps closer to the outlaw. 'What exactly is troubling you about this deal?'

'Who exactly is this Diamond Bob Casey character?' Smith asked. 'Is he a gunslinger and ya ain't telling us about it? I don't cotton to going up against no gunslinger.'

'I ain't too sure about that but I don't reckon he is a gunslinger.' Talbot was being honest for the first time as he thought about the look of the stranger whom he had seen enter the cantina. 'He don't look like a man that can handle a gun too well.'

Henry tilted his head. 'Ya seen him?'

Talbot nodded. 'Sure enough. He's in the cantina right now.'

'And ya want us to kill him?' Liam Davis asked.

'I'll kill him, but if I don't then I want your four guns to finish the critter off,' Talbot said blankly. 'Simple as that.'

49

'Why do ya want him dead, Tate?' Smith probed.

Talbot drew in his gut, clenched his right fist and swung his arm. The fist hit the outlaw square on the jaw. The whiskey glass flew from Smith's hand. Smith hit the wall behind him to the sound of shattering glass. He fell to his knees as blood poured from his mouth. His hand went for his gun but Talbot's hand was faster.

Within the blink of an eye Talbot had drawn and cocked his weapon and aimed it at Smith's head.

Frank Smith stared into the barrel of the cocked Colt .45.

'Easy, Tate! You win!'

Talbot nodded, spun his gun on his finger and dropped it expertly into his holster. He glared at the kneeling outlaw and then at the three others who sat watching.

'Two hundred bucks each,' Talbot snarled. 'No more questions and no more bucking. I'm still the boss of this outfit. Savvy?'

Smith slowly got to his feet. He rubbed off the blood from his mouth on his sleeve and watched as Talbot opened the door.

'C'mon!' Talbot growled. 'I want that varmint dead!'

Will Henry stood up. 'You heard him. C'mon! We gotta kill some joker in the cantina.'

The Davis brothers stood up, finished their drinks and rammed their cigars in their mouths.

'Let's do it,' Liam Davis said, and smiled.

'Nothing like a killing before supper to give a man an appetite,' his brother added.

The five men walked out of the room into the saloon and towards the swing doors. They had a man to kill. None of the quartet knew why but they still trailed their leader all the same.

Tate Talbot led them towards the cantina. It would prove to be the beginning of a long hard journey.

5

Hal Harper had not heard anything except his snorting horse and his own pounding heartbeat for more than a half-hour as he defiantly made his way through into the drifting haze. The gun in his hand had started to feel like a cudgel as weariness drowned him in his own sweat.

The sun was getting lower and he was walking straight into its blinding rays. Harper glanced back and saw the smoke of a campfire drifting up into the cloudless heavens. His hunters had indeed stopped to eat, he thought. He pressed on knowing that men with full bellies travelled more slowly than those with nothing but memories in their guts.

Eventually he could not walk another step and he paused beside the shoulder of his exhausted mount. He leaned against the muscular creature and lowered his gun.

'I'm done, boy,' he croaked.

Whatever had been making the elusive sounds earlier had ceased. Harper slid the Colt into its holster and tried to remain upright.

There was no breeze but he swayed all the same.

It was not as easy as it seemed to stay sure-footed when every drop of moisture had been sucked from your soul and the ground beneath your boots refused to quit moving.

The dense, foglike air confused his already weary eyes. If there was something to be seen, he sure could not locate it. Yet there had to be something out there. Something which had made the noises and lured him to it like flies to an outhouse.

Mustering what remained of his dwindling strength, Harper turned his head and looked back again. Hoofmarks and bootprints were all there was to be seen in the smooth dry sand. Once the five men started out after him again they would have no trouble following the trail he had left.

He rubbed a gloved hand over his sunburned neck and tried to create some spittle to moisten his throat. It was useless.

Again he forced himself away from the horse and gritted his teeth, He looked ahead once more.

'Anyone out there?' he croaked feebly.

Then he heard it.

The strange sound again. Closer now. Much closer.

Even in his bewildered condition Harper sensed that there was no danger from whatever was ahead of him. No bullets had come at him out of the heat haze.

Like a drunken man he began to stagger towards the noise he was starting to think he recognized. Step after faltering step he crossed the soft sand towards where his ears had told him the sound had come from.

But his legs began to buckle. They were not obeying his will any longer. He had to pause and steady himself every few yards. He had once been drunk in Laredo. Compared to this though, he had been sober.

'Where are you?' Harper's hoarse voice asked the mist. 'I ain't in no condition to hurt you. Show yourself!'

He had only just finished talking when his left boot got itself tangled up in something. He toppled and fell face first on to the sand. Whatever had tripped him up he neither cared nor worried about.

For what felt like a lifetime Harper lay trying to push himself back up on to his feet. But the sand was so welcoming he could not move. All he wanted to do was sleep. Sleep the sleep of the dead.

'OK, I quit! Stay dumb! I don't care no more,' Harper muttered into the sand. 'Hide, you yella dog! Hide!'

Then he felt the sand moving around him. He opened his eyes and saw legs. An instant later a hand rested on his shirt back.

Harper tried to raise his head but it

was useless. Whatever it was that had kept him on his feet for so long had evaporated like his sweat into the late-afternoon desert air.

'White eyes!' a voice said above him.

Harper blinked hard. Sand fell from his eyelashes as he stared at the feet of one of the men beside him. Although he had never seen a real Indian before he had heard the stories of the soft leather shoes they wore.

'Moccasins!' he gasped.

Then hands gripped his sore body, lifted it from the sand and began to carry him. He wanted to protest but was too tired to utter another word. His head dropped. His eyes stared at the sand below him. Then he saw the feet again. Four sets of feet. All with the same footwear.

Hal Harper wondered where they were taking him.

Then everything went dark as he fell into a pool of delirium.

A pool so deep there seemed to be no bottom to it.

6

They had been like a pack of rabid wolves by the time the evening air hit them. Tate Talbot led his four hired guns from the saloon with his gun already drawn and cocked. He was ready to put his once in a lifetime chance into action. There was no mercy in his heartless soul. Only greed. Within seconds of their crossing the wide street the five heavily armed men were outside the small cantina. Talbot was first to move close to the beaded drape which hung across the open doorway. The aroma of Mexican food filled his nostrils. His followers soon hung over his shoulders in readiness. Then the man with the tin star paused and held his free arm out wide as if to stop the others. This had to be fast and deadly, he had told himself. He had already decided to aim every one of the six bullets in his .45 at the stranger's head. He wanted there to be no argument that it was Diamond Bob Casey they had slain. The obvious age difference would be obliterated by lead. Hot, uncompromising lead.

But something had stopped the sheriff's progress. Something was wrong. Something had changed in the five or ten minutes since he had last seen the drifter dismount.

'What is it, Tate?' Will Henry had asked.

Talbot looked at the hitching pole and pointed. 'His horse is gone,' he replied.

Frank Smith glanced at the weathered wooden rail and then at Talbot. 'Ya sure there was a horse there?'

Talbot gritted his teeth and went to swing with his gun to smash the insolence off the face of the outlaw. Only Henry's hands prevented his angry boss from striking out at Smith for the second time in only minutes.

'Easy, Tate,' Will Henry implored.

'Don't waste no sweat on Frank, ya hear? He ain't worth it.'

Talbot looked into his top gun's eyes. He nodded. 'Yeah, Will. Ain't worth the effort.'

Liam Davis poked his head around the corner of the doorway and stared through the swaying beads into the busy cantina. He then turned and looked at Talbot.

'I see a stranger in there, Tate,' Davis said. 'Is that Diamond Bob Casey?'

Talbot brushed Smith out of his way and stood against the whitewashed doorway. His eyes narrowed. He looked in hard and long. The stranger whom he had seen ride into town only ten minutes earlier was indeed sitting down at a table with a plate of chilli before him. Talbot eased himself back.

'That's him OK,' Talbot nodded to the others.

Ken Davis shook his head. 'But what happened to his horse?'

'Yeah, that's what I can't figure. I saw him tie the damn thing up to that stinking pole,' Talbot insisted.

'It ain't here now.' Smith spat at the ground and sneered. 'Maybe the nag untied its tethers and went and rented a room in the hotel, Tate.'

Undaunted, Talbot checked his Colt. He then looked at his four men. His eyes told them what they had to do.

'It don't matter none. We're going in and we're going in shooting.'

Henry sighed. 'If that's what ya want, Tate, that's what we'll do.'

'Ya gonna go in first, Tate?' Smith taunted. 'Or are ya gonna be like one of them Yankee generals and hang back and take notes?'

'Damn right I'm going in first, Frank,' Talbot snarled back. 'I'm going in first like I've always done.'

The cantina was warm. The aroma of cooking filled the entire room. Hal Harper sat with his back to a low wall as the buxom female cook came close and placed a plate of fresh-baked bread down next to his chilli.

'Did your son take my horse to the

livery, ma'am?' Harper had asked innocently.

'*Sí, señor!*' She smiled, toying with the white lace trim of her bodice. 'Pepe is a good boy.'

Harper slid a silver dollar to the woman. 'That's for him when he gets back.'

'*Gracias, señor,*' she said as she picked up the coin and dropped in between her large breasts. 'I give to Pepe when he come back.'

Suddenly, as the words left her lips, the sound of raging men rushing through the beaded curtain into the cantina drew their eyes. As promised Tate Talbot was at the head of the five gunmen. His gun was first to unleash its fury and send a deadly bullet at the seated Harper. But as his four followers fanned their hammers, it was the stout cook between them who took the full impact of the venomous volley. She staggered and turned. Blood suddenly trailed from her as one after another lead bullet penetrated into her ample frame. She was being torn apart. She spun on her slippered feet on the tiled floor and started to fall.

Screams echoed all about the cantina. Some were cries of fury, others were shrieks of shocked horror.

A stunned Harper felt the warmth of her blood as it sprayed over him. He dragged his own Colt from its holster, ducked beneath the table and blasted back across the expanse of the room.

White-hot flashes spewed from the gun barrels in both directions in furious engagement. The cantina rocked under the deafening crescendo.

Within a very few seconds the peaceful cantina had filled with the acrid stench of gunfire. Clouds of grey smoke hung in the air.

It was Harper's only shield.

Harper threw himself to the floor as the stout cook hit the tiles. Again her body shook as more bullets cut into her now lifeless form. The silver coin rolled from her blood-soaked bodice towards him.

It was now crimson.

The youngster rolled back towards a massive cooking range and then found a small whitewashed wall to give him cover. He pushed himself up against it as more bullets tore across the room. Plaster exploded everywhere and covered Harper. He cocked his gun hammer again.

Harper looked around the side of the low wall and blasted his Colt again.

Another volley of lead smashed into the iron cooking-range behind him. Harper ducked as shrapnel bounced off the walls and cascaded over him.

Then, dusting the debris off his screwed-up eyes, he saw the open window to his left. His mind raced. He had no idea why the five gunmen had opened up on him and yet they had. The piteous body of the female was evidence of that. He knew he had to escape or he would join her.

Scrambling on to his knees the young man inhaled deeply. He then rose up from his hiding-place. Only the thick smoke masked his movement from the eyes of his attackers. He sprang and leapt like a puma through the gap in the white wall.

Harper hit the sand outside the window, rolled over and then began to run into the unlit alleys. How long it would take them to discover his flight he could not know, but Harper did not waste a second thought on the subject. Their bullets had not even grazed him and he wanted to keep it that way. He did not stop running until he arrived at the livery stable and found his horse again.

No man had ever saddled a horse as speedily as Harper had done that dark night. Within minutes he had mounted and spurred and ridden away from Senora.

Had he known that the five men behind him would continue to chase him for the next two days into a merciless desert, Harper might have chosen to remain in Senora and fight.

But he had spurred instead.

Foresight was a gift he, like so many others, had never been blessed with.

★ ★ ★

Like the ticking of a clock the sound grew more and more annoying to the man lying helplessly on his back. Harper battled with the nightmares which taunted him until he eventually won and opened his eyes. For a moment he just stared upward. The day had ended and had been replaced by a million stars twinkling like jewels on a black velvet cloth. Harper wondered how long he had been asleep.

Then the sound which had dogged and taunted him for so long before he had at last fallen unconscious became obvious. His eyes darted to his right and he saw it.

His eyes focused upon the wheel atop an upturned wagon. As the sand beneath the weathered framework of the ancient prairie schooner shifted, the wheel moved. With no grease remaining between hub and axle the noise continued.

An ear-splitting noise.

Suddenly Harper realized that his throat was no longer dry. He raised a hand and touched his face. It had been washed free of the sand that had stung like a nest of loco hornets for so long, and had been covered in some sort of salve.

Harper raised himself up on an elbow. The sight which met him reminded him of the moments just before he had lost his fight with the blackness which had overwhelmed him.

He blinked hard.

It made no difference. They were still there.

Six Indians sat close to him. Their colourful ponies were tied up close by and his own horse's reins were secured to the tailgate of the wagon.

'You helped me,' Harper said with more than a hint of surprise in his voice. 'How come?'

Five of the braves remained seated

like carved statues. The sixth rose and crawled to the side of the weak Harper.

'They no have your tongue,' the brave said. 'I only one who speak your tongue. You sick like lost dog. We help.'

Harper stared at the man beside him. Although he had never met an Indian before he had seen many photographic images of various tribes. This man and his companions did not seem to fit into any likeness that he could recall.

'Are you an Apache?'

The man shook his head angrily. 'No Apache! We have no name. We come from the place where the eagle soars high and we live higher in the face of the golden mountain.'

Harper sat upright. 'I don't understand.'

The brave pointed south. 'There is our land. We live there all time since Great Spirit made us.'

Harper still did not understand. He looked around him. The dunes surrounded them on three sides. Suddenly he recalled the five riders who had been after him for two days. He grabbed the hand of the brave.

'Have you seen the other men?' He held up his own hand and pointed to his fingers. 'Five bad men!'

The Indian nodded. 'They sleep.'

Harper heaved a big sigh. 'Good.'

'Why they hunt you?'

'I don't know, friend,' Harper replied honestly. 'They want me dead though, and no mistake.'

The Indian nodded. 'Apache hunt and kill my people. We know not why.'

Harper was anxious. He rubbed his neck. 'I have to get away from here but I'm plumb lost.'

'You fit to travel, White Eyes?' The voice was low and concerned. 'You want we take you to better place?'

'I reckon so.'

'We travel by stars.' The warrior stood and then helped Harper up on to his feet. 'We give you and pony water when you sick. Desert cannot kill if you have water.'

'I thank you.' Harper ran a hand

along the horse he had thought would be buzzard bait by now. The creature looked fresh and able to continue their journey. Harper looked at the Indian brave again. 'Where did you get water in this desert?'

The Indian smiled. 'Water all over if you know where to look for it.'

'All I see is sand,' Harper confessed. 'I must be pretty dumb.'

The Indian nodded in agreement. 'We ride now.'

7

For more than seven hours the caravan of horses moved slowly through the dunes beneath the bright moon. An eerie silence filled the air as the soft terrain muffled the shod and unshod hoofs. During the long trek one of the other braves had spotted some sort of deer. With a swiftness and accuracy which astounded Harper the Indian had produced a bow and sent an arrow across 300 yards and killed the creature. It had been gutted and thrown across the hindquarters of the brave's pony within minutes of the kill. Only then did Harper notice several other dead animals on the rest of the ponies. This must be a hunting party seeking game to return to their mysterious homeland, Harper thought.

The Indian who had spoken to Harper led them. Like an ancient mariner out in the middle of an uncharted ocean he used the stars to lead him back to the place from which they had originally set out. For the first time in more than two days the young drifter felt safe.

Whoever these strange Indians were, he concluded, they were friendly. They were not the savages he had heard tell of by those who had only read about the West in dime novels.

Hal Harper wondered where they were headed.

He also wondered if he would ever be able to return to the place he had once called home. A place far to the east of the Pecos river.

But he would gladly remain with these people if it meant that he would not find himself in another cruel battle like the one he had been involved in back at Senora. He had never had to fight for his life before and he did not wish to repeat the experience.

As mile followed mile a thousand thoughts filtered through his mind. But, unlike those that had tormented him before he had been saved from certain death by these six strangely dressed men with long black hair, his thoughts were no longer dark.

Now he could actually imagine surviving in this desert.

He raised himself in his stirrups and looked around the strange, bluish landscape. The dunes were now thinning out and far ahead he could see towering spires of rock.

Harper looked at the rider ahead of him. A single feather was plaited into the back of his mane of hair. It floated on the warm air and danced across the man's shoulders.

Who were these people?

Where was this land of theirs?

The description of it being the place where eagles soared high in a sky above where they lived in a golden mountain made no sense to Harper. Perhaps, he thought, the Indian had meant something else. But what?

Yet the thought of them living in a

golden mountain intrigued the young horseman. Could it be true? Was there even the remotest of chances that it was true?

So many questions filled his mind. So few answers.

He kept his horse aimed after the lead rider. It was obvious that the man knew where he was headed.

Harper eased his mount alongside the pony.

The Indian pulled back on his rope reins and stopped his pony. Harper drew rein and stopped his own horse. The five others encircled them.

For a few seconds the Indians spoke to one another in their strange language and then the lead rider looked at Harper.

'New day soon,' he said, pointing at the horizon.

Again, Harper stood for a moment in his stirrups and stared out across the moonlit dunes to where the towering rocks stood like elongated stone fingers. Fingers which pointed at the very stars themselves.

'What White Eyes look for?'

'I thought there was a lake out here someplace,' Harper said. 'I could have sworn I saw a lake earlier.'

The Indian smiled. 'Desert play tricks with you. It alive. It play and make you come to it. Then it kill. Desert have many ways to kill.'

A chill crept up Harper's spine. He knew what his companion meant. There were lakes that only existed in the minds of those the desert tormented. He knew that he had come close to becoming just another pile of bleached bones. He shook again.

'Why'd we stop, friend?' Harper asked.

'Horses need drink. Braves need drink.' The Indian dropped from the back of his pony. The others followed suit.

Harper looked all around them. 'But there ain't no water hereabouts.'

The Indian told his fellow braves what Harper had said. They all began to laugh.

'Hey! What's your name?' Harper asked the Indian.

'I am Talka.'

'I'm called Hal.'

'Hal.' Talka repeated the name and then knelt down on the soft sand. His large hands started to smooth the sand away in wide, well-practised strokes.

'What you doing, Talka?' Harper asked.

There was no reply. Within a few seconds the answer became obvious. A thin, almost perfectly round stone was revealed. Talka looked at his fellow braves, muttered a few words and they all knelt down beside him. Each gripped the rim of the stone and began to drag it sideways.

Harper felt his jaw drop in amazement. He stepped closer and stared into the hole. Even the eerie moonlight could not hide the sight of the water rippling. Water where the reflection of the large moon danced.

'A well? Out here?'

Talka looked up. 'Water.'

Harper nodded. 'I'll be damned!'

The Indians went to their ponies and pulled the large water bags from off the animals' shoulders. One by one they dropped them into the cold, fresh liquid until they were filled.

'Like Talka said,' the Indian explained. 'You have to know where to look, White Eyes Hal.'

'But how?' Harper could not comprehend.

'Many moons ago my people had wells all over this land,' Talka explained. 'There were trees then. We always protected the water. Then the desert came. Slow at first. Then fast. The sand killed everything but not the water.'

Harper watched as the Indians watered their ponies and put the bags back over the shoulders of the creatures. He helped Talka return the flat stone over the waterhole and push the sand back over it.

'You have more of these waterholes, Talka?'

The Indian smiled. 'Many.'

They mounted again and drew their reins up to their chests. Talka pointed at the horizon. The very edge of the desert was starting to show signs of a new day. It appeared as though a glowing fire was out there just where the land met the sky. A fire which would soon erupt and send its light hurtling across the desert.

'We must go,' Talka said. 'Not safe out here when sun comes back.'

Suddenly the distinctive sound of rifle fire broke the desert's silence. One of the Indians screamed out in agony and slumped over the neck of his mount.

Harper drew his Colt and spun his horse full circle in a vain attempt to see who had fired the shot.

'I thought you said them five critters that was hunting me were asleep, Talka? They must have trailed us here.'

'Not white men.' Talka reached across from his own pony and grabbed the mane of the wounded Indian's mount.

Harper closed the distance between them. 'Not white men? Then who?'

Talka pointed.

The youngster looked.

A score of mounted figures were lined up on a dune 200 yards to their left. The sunlight sped over the desert and crept up the dune. The twenty horsemen were then bathed in the red, glowing illumination.

It was a terrifying sight.

'Who are they?' Harper yelled.

'They Apache.'

'Why they shooting at us?'

'They war party. They want our food.' Talka replied hurriedly. 'They kill us to get it, Hal.'

Harper cocked his gun hammer and blasted his .45 at the distant Apaches. They did not flinch. They knew that only a rifle could span the distance between them.

'Damn! I ain't got the range,' Harper said.

'We go.' Talka thrust his heels into the sides of his pony and began to ride hard. The others followed. Harper spurred in pursuit.

Then more rifle fire came.

'Ride into the sun!' Talka ordered his followers.

The seven horsemen rode into the sun.

8

Dawn was greeted by the sound of Apache rifle fire. It travelled unchecked for miles across a landscape of sand dunes like the rumbling of distant thunderclaps. Its hideous clamour filled the dry desert air around the camp where Talbot and his four henchmen had bedded down for the night and still slept. It was the youngest of Talbot's men, Ken Davis, who awoke first and jumped to his feet with his six-shooter in his hand.

Dazed and confused, Davis looked all around them as his startled companions clambered out of their bedrolls and got to their feet.

'What ya shooting at, Ken?' Talbot growled.

'It weren't me that was shooting, Tate,' Davis replied as even more shots could be heard. 'But somebody out there sure is.'

'We got us some company by the sounds of it, Tate,' Smith sneered.

Again more shots rang out far in the distance. The five men looked at one another. None of them could understand who in this unholy place was wasting so much lead.

'That's rifle shots, Tate,' Will Henry said firmly. 'Maybe someone else is after our Casey!'

'Yep! It was rifle shots all right, Will,' Talbot agreed as he walked out from the shadow of the dune into the bright sunlight and shielded his eyes from the low rising sun, 'and they're coming from that direction.'

Smith dusted himself off. 'Who do ya figure would be firing rifles out here?'

'It sure wouldn't be Diamond Bob Casey,' Liam Davis said bluntly as he plucked his bedroll off the sand.

'He ain't even got a carbine,' Henry added. 'If he had one he'd have bin able to pick us off by now. Who the hell is it out there?'

Talbot looked at his men.

'Saddle up! We're gonna find out if somebody else is trying to kill our Casey. If they are then we'll kill them.'

Smith lifted his bedroll and paused beside Talbot. His eyes burned into the larger man.

Talbot turned to face Smith. 'What's eatin' you, Frank?'

'How much is this Casey worth dead or alive, Tate?' Smith asked coyly.

'What ya mean?'

'He must be worth a hell of a lot.' Smith nodded. 'You wouldn't have brung us all the way out here into this desert if that dude wasn't worth a small fortune.'

Talbot said nothing.

'Or maybe it ain't a small fortune,' Smith continued. 'Maybe he's worth a real big one. Am I right, Tate?'

Talbot looked at the others. They were all waiting for the answer as keenly as Smith was.

'He's worth a tidy sum.'

'How much?'

Talbot's mind raced. 'Thousands.'

'How many thousands?' Smith pressed.

'OK. Casey's worth ten grand,' Talbot lied.

'I figure that's two grand apiece, Tate,' Smith said. 'Not the stinking two hundred ya wanted to pay us.

Reluctantly, Talbot nodded to the others. 'OK, I'll split the reward with you boys, even, like Frank here wants.'

Smith wandered to their horses. He winked at Henry and threw his blanket on the back of his horse.

'Ya don't want to rile Tate, Frank,' Henry whispered. 'Tate ain't the sort ya want to rile.'

'Quit grumbling, old-timer,' Smith said, as he lifted his saddle and threw it on to the back of his horse. 'I just made us an extra eighteen hundred dollars apiece.'

Talbot walked across to his horse and untied the reins which had kept the animal from straying through the hours of darkness. Without saying a word the man with the tin star on his shirt began

83

to ready his mount for the next part of their pursuit.

Will Henry inhaled deeply. 'I'd have settled for the two hundred dollars Tate was offering.'

'I got us a lot more money, old-timer,' Smith said with a twisted smile. 'I for one will enjoy spending that extra dough.'

'If ya live long enough to spend it, Frank.' Will Henry glanced at Talbot and then back at Smith. 'I've known Tate a tad longer than you. He ain't the sort to cross and you just crossed him. He won't forget that in a coon's age.'

Smith pulled the cinch strap from under the belly of his mount and threaded it through its buckle.

'I ain't scared.'

Henry picked his saddle off the sand. 'I am.'

9

Blazing shafts of ghostlike rifle bullets cut through the morning air in deafening succession. Plumes of white-hot sand kicked heavenward as the shells failed to strike their retreating targets. The twenty Apaches swarmed like soldier ants over the hot sand dunes in chase of their prey. Again and again their rifles spewed out deadly lead as they screamed out their chilling war cries. It mattered nothing to the Apaches that six of the seven men they were pursuing were also Indians. They were not Apaches.

In their hearts this was their land. Apache land. Anyone within its confines was sentenced to death without a single word ever being uttered.

All laws here were as they had always been.

They were unwritten, but just as lethal.

After years of being moved from one hostile environment to even worse reservations, the twenty braves had rebelled and left the confines of their enforced new home.

They would not be moved on again. They would no longer be treated like livestock. They would die rather than allow their dignity to be eroded further. The Apaches had a saying: 'It is a good day to fight, it is a good day to die.'

To them they were no longer living. They were existing. Death held no fear for men on the very edge of extermination. There was nothing left to lose. They had already lost everything except their defiance.

Feverishly the braves galloped into the low morning sun firing their rifles at targets they could barely see as the merciless rays of the blinding orb faced them.

But unlike so many others who had drifted into this unholy land, Talka knew how to survive most things it challenged him with. Being attacked by braves far more heavily armed than those he led was just one of them. He knew that if he kept the sun in the eyes of those who followed them, it would act as a shield.

It was said that only the Devil and the Apache could survive in such a hostile terrain as the desert. It was not true. Six of the seven riders the Apaches chased were also more than capable of existing in this ferocious land.

Only Apache bullets could prevent them from living through another day.

The seven horsemen had ridden for nearly two miles through the soft unforgiving sand as the Apache war party closed in on them with every stride of their small, fit ponies. Hal Harper spurred his mount yet he could barely keep up with his companions' far smaller animals.

They were built for this territory. His long-legged horse with its shod hoofs was not. The Indian ponies thundered low to the sand with their bareback riders gripping and steering them with muscular legs.

Harper rode high with the burden of his saddle weighing down his mount. As the bullets got closer, Harper held on to his saddle horn with his left hand, leaned against the neck of his horse and aimed his six-shooter under the horse's throat.

As the panting animal beneath him turned to follow the tail of the last pony, Harper saw that the Apaches were now within range of his .45.

He squeezed the trigger.

He saw one of the braves in the middle of the following pack punched from his pony by the sheer impact of his lead.

'Got ya!' Harper said through gritted teeth.

The rest of the Apaches continued their chase. Now they seemed to be even louder than before. Now they seemed to be forcing their ponies to find even greater pace. Now they were getting close.

Dangerously close.

Harper pulled the hammer of his weapon back again. It locked into position. He closed one eye and fired again.

This time his bullet was not true. He saw one of the braves buckle but the Apache did not fall. Defiantly he kept riding on and on.

Harper swung back up on to his saddle and spurred harder than he had ever done before.

The horse responded.

'Keep going, boy!' Harper yelled at his mount.

Like the faithful creature it had always been, the horse thundered through the sand and caught up with Talka and his fellow Indians.

As all seven rode up a sandy rise, Talka gestured to two of his fellow braves. They cut the carcasses of the dead animals free from behind them. The stiff bodies of the game fell and bounced on the sand. Harper knew that Talka was trying to see if the Apaches were hungry enough to settle for a third of the Indians' hunting triumphs.

Half of the Apaches drew rein and stopped when they reached the fresh gutted game. But nine of them continued after the seven riders ahead of them.

A volley of shots rang out from the Apache rifles. Red tapers spat all about the riders. Standing in his stirrups, Harper felt something brush past his left arm, which started to burn. He glanced at it. Then he saw the blood soaking his shirtsleeve. He had been winged, but there was no pain. Only a feeling of burning.

'White Eyes!' Talka called back.

Harper screwed up his eyes against the sand that cut into his face from the hoofs of the fleeing ponies around his own. He saw Talka point to their left and then turn the neck of his mount brutally.

They all followed suit.

The soft sand was replaced with a gritty trail which led alongside a rocky overhang.

Talka called out. It was not words but a guttural call which chilled Harper to the bone. They all closed up behind the lead rider as he yelled out again.

Suddenly the ground fell away.

All seven mounts leapt into a place where the sun had yet to reach. They started to fall through the darkness.

Their masters leaned back and clung to their reins as the horses clawed at the very air itself.

Harper closed his eyes and waited.

It was a wait which seemed to last forever.

10

They had fallen for more than forty feet into a deep dark chasm and hit a slope of soft sand with brutal force. The sheer impact of the unseen ground beneath the hoofs of the animals sent each of the horsemen flying over the necks of the mounts. Every ounce of wind was knocked out of the horses. They staggered and then fell on to their knees. Their masters fared little better. Each of them had landed hard and just lay where they had fallen trying to suck air back into their bruised bodies.

High above them they could see the whooping figures gathering at the very edge of where the trail ceased to exist.

It was Talka who managed to rise from the sand first. Like the true leader he obviously was he checked all his men and their ponies for injuries. Only when satisfied that they had survived without any broken bones did he move to Harper.

Harper accepted the hand and got to his feet. He was about to speak when Talka turned his back and returned to the one Indian who had been wounded by an Apache rifle bullet as they had fled the wrath of those who had pursued them.

Dusting himself down, Harper took some deep breaths and walked to where Talka knelt beside the only Indian who had not risen from the sand where they had all landed seconds earlier.

'Is he OK, Talka?'

The Indian got back to his feet. Even the shadows could not hide the concern etched into his features.

'Not good, Hal,' came the simple reply.

'This ain't no place to be wounded in,' Harper said, casting his eyes around the dark rocky walls which rose high to where they had ridden from. 'Wherever this damn place is.'

Talka signalled to his other braves to

check their ponies more thoroughly. They did as commanded without uttering a single word.

Harper rubbed his arm. The pain suddenly erupted.

'Damn it all!' Harper snarled quietly. 'I forgot they winged me as well.'

Talka gave the graze a quick look and shook his head. 'It not bad, White Eyes. Bullet just cut skin. My brother is hurt bad. Bullet in him. Need to be cut out soon.'

'How soon?'

'Very soon.'

Harper turned and looked at his horse. Its forelegs were buried deep in the soft sand where it had landed. Defiantly it vainly struggled to free itself. The drifter moved close to it and ran a concerned hand across his mount's neck.

'Easy, boy. I'll get you up on your feet.'

'Horse OK?' Talka asked Harper.

'Shaken up a tad,' Harper answered. 'But I reckon he'll be fine as soon as I get him standing on some firm ground.'

'Good,' Talka nodded. 'We need ponies OK for long ride back to my land.'

The bruised and battered braves picked up the expertly butchered game and water sacks and started to return them to the shoulders and backs of their unsteady animals.

Harper used his hands to shovel the sand away from the legs of his tall horse. At last the animal managed to stand.

The rocky confines the seven men found themselves in soon began to resound with the Apaches' chants coming from far above them. Nervously, Harper grabbed the bridle of his horse and led it closer to the safety of the rockface. He looked upward and then saw the fearsome warriors shouting down from their high vantage point.

Talka moved unseen by the Apache warriors through the shadows to the side of the troubled Harper. His hand rested on the younger man's shoulder.

'Be unafraid, White Eyes Hal,' he said firmly.

'That's not as easy as it sounds, Talka.' Harper swallowed hard.

Talka waved signals to his keen-eyed followers. They seemed to understand his every gesture. The brave then looked back at the young man he had taken under his wing.

'Apaches no like dark place,' Talka told him. 'They not come down here. We safe for time.'

'They don't come down into this place?' Harper repeated the statement. 'Why not?'

'The spirits of their dead live here,' Talka said.

Harper raised his eyebrows. 'I don't savvy.'

Talka led the young man across the sandy slope to a spot almost directly below the place from where they had driven their mounts. The older man knelt and then scooped some sand away with his left hand. Harper gasped, then dropped down on to one knee beside his benefactor.

The eyes of the young drifter narrowed. He stared in disbelief at the bones and then saw a skull. He looked at Talka open-mouthed.

'Is this one of their kind?' he asked.

Talka nodded. 'This Apache. They used to use this place to drop their dead into. It is said that the spirits of a hundred warriors live in this place.'

Harper gulped even harder. 'So they bury their dead here.'

'And they think it is a sacred place.' Talka added. 'But Talka no think this 'happy hunting ground', White Eyes Hal.'

'Your tribe ain't afraid?'

Talka stood again. 'The dead Apaches cannot hurt us. Only the living Apaches can do that.'

Hal Harper returned to his full height. His eyes were drawn back up to the Apaches as they continued to spit out their verbal venom at those they believed had defiled their holy place.

'You told me not to be scared, Talka. I'm sorry, but I ain't never bin so afraid in all my days. How are we gonna get out of this place alive?'

'There are many trails out from here.' Talka said. 'We only need to take one of them.'

Harper nodded. 'How come them Apaches ain't fired their rifles down here at us? I'd have thought they'd sure want to kill us more now than when we was up there in the fresh air.'

'They do not wish to offend their ghosts.' The Indian shrugged and led the taller man back to the wounded Indian who still lay in the sand. He shook his head slowly and then turned to one of his other companions. He said something in a low hushed tone and then ran his fingers through his mane of long dark hair. His eyes glanced upward before returning to Harper.

'My brother is dead,' he said quietly.

'I'm sorry,' Harper replied.

The other braves lifted the body up from the sand and then laid it carefully across the back of the black-and-white pony between a water sack and the lifeless body of a deer.

Talka watched silently as they used rawhide strips to tie the body of his brother securely.

'You ain't gonna bury your brother here, Talka?' Harper asked his friend.

'Not with Apache bones, Hal,' Talka said heavily. 'We take him back to our land and give him to the wind and the sun. His dust will travel to places we cannot go.'

Harper had no idea what the Indian beside him meant but knew that if he lived long enough, he would eventually discover the answer to all his unasked questions.

★ ★ ★

They rode two by two in a column more than a hundred yards in length. Eighteen dust-caked troopers were being led by a veteran of more than five Indian campaigns. Captain Eli Forbes

99

was one of the old school of cavalry officers, straight-backed and grim-faced. Few had ever seen a smile cross his weathered features. In fact few had ever seen any emotion on the face of the officer who thought that any sign of humanity was a sign of weakness. His troop had travelled a long way in chase of the twenty or so Apache bucks who had escaped from the reservation forty miles east of the sterile desert they now found themselves in. They had left Fort Myers seven weeks earlier with five heavily laden packmules in tow.

Their trek had been a hard one. The Apaches were unlike so many other tribes that Forbes had faced during his long and illustrious career. Most Indians sought out and found land which was better than the one they had left behind them. Not the Apaches. They were hardened souls who seemed able to take even the harshest of terrains in their stride.

Forbes knew that each day, after they had tracked the men they were charged with bringing back to the designated reservation, the Apaches would simply alter direction. The twenty painted riders would go west and then south and then west again. It made no sense to the military mind of the army captain. There was no logic in it. They would be headed for water one day and then back-track into what seemed to be a place where nothing could exist.

Yet the Apaches navigated the arid landscape and somehow remained alive.

Forbes knew that his was a mission most would have considered impossible. For years men had tried and failed to capture the famed Apache leader Geronimo. A fortune had been spent in a vain attempt to capture the wily Indian and all it had achieved was a lot of dead trackers and even more dead horses.

Forbes had begun to wonder if these twenty or so Apaches might be like their legendary leader. Could they escape capture indefinitely?

It was beginning to appear so.

There were no marked borders in this land. The expert cavalryman had no idea whether they were still in America or had ventured into the forbidden Mexico where his gold braid meant nothing. Yet he continued to forge on regardless. He had been told to capture the braves by any means possible. Forbes was quite willing to kill them all if that was what it took to establish his authority.

Mile after mile and day after day it was becoming obvious not only to Forbes but to his enlisted followers that they could not possibly still be on American soil. Yet he continued to lead them onward.

Forbes raised a hand and stopped his troop. His chest heaved as his lungs tried to suck air into them. Sergeant Bruno Coogan rode to the side of his superior officer and looked at the man whose tanned face stared out at the white featureless land ahead of them. Even the trail of their scout was no longer visible.

'We gonna make camp, sir?' Coogan asked hoarsely.

Forbes nodded slowly. 'For a few hours, Coogan. Get some coffee and vittles cooked up for the men. When we've eaten we'll continue.'

Coogan looked at the sand ahead of them. Sand which rose in whirls as a mocking breeze skimmed the surface of the ground. If there had been tracks to follow, he thought, they were long gone now. His wrinkled eyes turned and focused on Forbes. He had served with the man for ten long years and had never seen him buckle. Even now Forbes remained as rigid as he always had been.

'You sure the scout went thataway, sir?'

'I'm sure,' Forbes retorted stiffly.

'How?' Coogan scratched his whiskered face. A face in total contrast to the clean-shaven one of his officer. 'There ain't no tracks any place.'

Forbes looked at his sergeant. 'Trust me! I know where they're headed. It came to me last night just after we bedded down. When the scout returns he will confirm my theory.'

Coogan leaned closer. 'The men are starting to get a mite edgy, sir. This desert ain't fit for men.'

'The Apaches are headed to a place that I believe is called the Devil's Elbow.' Forbes uttered the words quietly. 'I'm led to believe that this was where they originally came from. Their ancestral home, if you like. Mark my words, that is where we shall find them.'

'But Apaches are nomads, sir,' Coogan said. 'They ain't from no place. They just wander around killing good Bible-reading folks for the joy of it.'

Forbes shook his head. 'You're wrong, my friend. Even the Apache have roots. When we get there we shall find them.'

'And kill 'em?'

Forbes took in a deep breath. 'If necessary.'

★ ★ ★

There were few sights which could have frightened men as rugged and seasoned as Tate Talbot was. Yet this one did. The five riders had galloped across the soft shifting sand for more than five miles when, after managing to ride up a mountainous dune, Talbot suddenly saw the group of Apaches ahead of his small troop. The wide brim of his battered sweat-stained Stetson cut out the sun's fury but he could do nothing to prevent the instinctive panic that almost stopped his heart from beating.

He dug his boots into his stirrups, hauled back on his reins and brought his mount to a sudden halt.

The Davis brothers had only just reached the top of the dune when they were forced to follow suit and abruptly stop their horses behind their leader. Smith and Henry dragged rein and eased their mounts to either side of Talbot's snorting charge.

A cloud of dry sand drifted away from the dune's crest and floated across the blue, cloudless sky. It was more than enough to alert the eyes of those who were at home in this godless place.

Will Henry raised a gloved hand and used its shade to stare at the Apaches who were already staring back at the sun-baked intruders behind them.

Talbot steadied his uneasy horse and looked down at the Apaches who had been gathering up the dead carcasses of desert deer dropped by Tarka's braves as they had fled the volley of bullets which chased them even faster than the Apaches' ponies.

'Damn it all, boys!' Talbot snarled loudly in angry confusion. 'Apaches! I never figured on it being Apaches that was doing all the shooting.'

'And they done seen us, Tate,' Smith added.

'What they got down there, Tate?' Henry asked. 'Is that Diamond Bob Casey they're hauling across the sand?'

'Nope. Looks like deer to me,' Talbot spat.

Liam Davis swung his mount full circle in an attempt to prevent it from fleeing the merciless rays of the blinding sun.

'I'm for high-tailin' it out of here, Tate,' the eldest of the Davis boys chipped in. 'I don't mind chasing and killing a white *hombre* but I draws the line at mixing punches with savages.'

Ken Davis held his reins up to his chest and kept his own horse in check. He looked at the ten or so Indians below them and then back at Talbot.

'Liam's talking sense,' he told Talbot. 'We ain't gonna last long if'n we tangles with Apaches.'

'Ya scared?' Talbot growled.

'Yep!' both Davis brothers said at exactly the same time.

'But Casey's tracks head on straight through there.' Talbot pointed at the deep churned-up sand they had been following for more than thirty minutes. 'We gonna let a bunch of painted heathens scare us off? Ya willing to lose ten grand in crisp fresh-minted greenbacks?'

Will Henry leaned closer to his

leader. 'We're outnumbered two to one, Tate. If'n it was white men I'd not be worried but I've never gone up against that many Injuns before.'

Talbot looked at Henry. 'Not you as well? I thought that you'd have the guts to try, Will.'

'I just don't want my guts spread out all over this sand for buzzard bait,' Henry admitted.

'Let's ride out of here,' Ken Davis begged.

Smith looked at the youngest member of their small band and waved a knowing finger. 'Ya think that our nags can outrun Apache ponies, Ken boy?'

Ken looked at his brother and then Henry. Both men were shaking their heads in answer. He then returned his eyes to Smith.

'Ya mean we gotta fight them?'

'Better than a back full of arrows or lead,' Smith winked.

Talbot looked heavenward for a second and then back at his four men. Against his own better judgement he decided to use his last wild card to try to buy their help.

'OK! OK! What if I was to pay ya all four thousand dollars apiece?'

Frank Smith blinked hard. 'How?'

Talbot turned his head. 'I lied about the reward money. Casey's worth twenty thousand dollars, not ten thousand.'

Frank Smith smiled wide. 'Ya as crooked as I am, Tate. I like that in a man.'

'Yep,' Talbot nodded. 'I thought ya might.'

Smith eyed the others. 'I'm willing to to try and kill me some Apaches for that kind of dough. What about you, boys?'

The Davis brothers remained silent.

Henry shook his head. 'Look at them young bucks down there, Frank. They all got at least ten years on us. How can we get the better of any of them? Back in Senora on Main Street maybe, but here?'

'Four grand, Will,' Smith gushed

greedily. 'That's worth dying for.'

Talbot adjusted himself on his saddle. He raised his gloved right hand and pointed at the Apaches. They were moving to their ponies fast.

'Make up ya minds, boys. Ya ain't got much time.'

Liam Davis shook his head.

'I'm for riding.'

Before his brother could open his mouth a sound cut through the dry morning air. It was one that they knew only too well. Rifle fire could never be mistaken for anything else.

But recognition came a fraction of a heartbeat too late. Ken Davis was lifted off his saddle as his chest exploded under the impact of the small lead bullet. Blood splattered over the other riders. Davis fell limply to his right and hit the ground hard. His left boot remained caught in its stirrup. The sand went red as a crimson river poured from the deep bullet wound in his chest.

'Ken!' Liam screamed out in horror.

'Them Apaches have got carbines, Tate!' Henry shouted.

The four remaining horsemen steadied their mounts and watched in horror as Ken Davis's horse galloped down the dune towards the group of well-armed Apaches. A trail of gore was left in the hoof-prints punched into the sand.

Talbot leaned back and grabbed the wooden stock of his own Winchester. He pulled it free of its long saddle scabbard and brought it up to his shoulder. He cocked its mechanism and fired into the heart of the gathered warriors. One of the ponies fell on to the sand. Talbot quickly fired a second shot. This time it was one of the Apaches who fell.

'Good shot!' Smith praised as he drew one of his Colts and fired down into the heart of the Indians.

'C'mon!' Talbot urged. 'Kill the varmints!'

'What we gonna do?' Liam Davis screamed above the sound of rifle- and gun-fire.

There was only one thing they could do.

As bullets cut through the air all around the riders the four horsemen spurred and thundered down the dune atop their fevered mounts and started to fire their arsenal of varied weaponry at the Apaches.

A sickening cloud of gunsmoke enveloped the desert as both sides blasted at one another.

Within seconds the white sand had been stained scarlet.

11

With reins gripped between their teeth and blazing weapons in their hands, the quartet of horsemen thundered down the dune towards the small group of Apaches. They spurred and fired with equal ferocity as their already lathered-up mounts ploughed through the sand towards the rifles of their adversaries. As he had always done, Talbot led from the front.

The desert shook as rifles and six-guns spewed out their lethal lead from both sides. The Apaches had been quick to reach their ponies and the rifles they had managed to acquire on their journey from the reservation. Yet the guns of Talbot and his outlaws had been equal to them.

Shafts of red-hot tapers cut through the dry air from the riders' weapons into the Indians and their mounts.

Apaches fell wounded and dead into the sand. But the deadly traffic of bullets was not one-way. It moved in both directions. The rifles of the young Indians who managed to avoid the bullets of the horsemen were just as vicious and just as accurate.

Will Henry had not wanted this fight. But he had followed Talbot anyway. It had proved to be the right thing to do on more occasions than he could recall. But this time he should have listened to the gnawing in his craw and not the valiant words that had been spat from the mouth of the man with the tin star. This time Henry should have high-tailed it as the Davis boys had urged.

It was unclear how many bullets hit the eldest of the outlaws before he finally slumped in his saddle and gasped his last utterances. Even though its master was on his way to Hell itself, Henry's horse kept charging on. As Talbot kept cranking the lever of his Winchester and blasting back from his galloping mount he had seen Henry riddled with lead beside him. Talbot was fast to react.

Casting his empty rifle aside, the leader of the small outlaw gang drew his own horse level with that of his already dead friend. He reached across and grabbed the bridle of the wide-eyed mount and pulled it close to his own.

Now Will Henry would be his shield.

Steering his and Henry's horses towards the churned-up trail he and his men had followed for over two days, Talbot dragged one of his Colts from its holster and cocked its hammer. He would not waste a single bullet, for there was no way that he could reload his guns when travelling at break-neck speed.

The dust of fine sand was blinding to both sides in the furious battle. It masked the eyes of the gunmen from their targets but it also protected them from their foes' lead.

Frank Smith had fared better than Henry.

He was still alive.

Being a man who valued his own life above all others, Smith had managed to drive his own horse away from where the Indians were gathered. He would let Talbot and Henry soak up their bullets as he forged on in chase of the man he now knew was worth $20,000 dead or alive.

Smith had ridden low over his saddle to make himself a smaller target for the Apaches' bullets. Hanging across the shoulders of a galloping mount did indeed make him far smaller target but it did nothing to reduce the size of the mount beneath his saddle.

His luck did not last long.

The Apaches might have been young but they possessed all the skills and cunning of their elders. They blasted their rifles at the horse instead. It was a target that even a blind man could have found.

Two of the kneeling Apaches turned their carbines on to the horse beneath Smith. He heard the shots and then felt the animal buckle under him.

It happened quickly.

One second the horse was thundering at top pace and then next it was hitting the sand so hard it sent its master flying through the air. The horse cartwheeled and crashed.

Liam Davis should have listened to his own advice. He should have turned and spurred away from the near-naked men covered in war paint. Yet even he had swallowed Talbot's sugar. He had blindly followed his three companions with his guns blazing at the Apaches.

Perhaps it had been revenge which had made him spur and start to fire his guns so feverishly. He had just seen his kid brother killed with a single well-aimed shot beside him. He had then seen the body of his brother dragged down the dune by the terrified horse and tossed around like a rag doll, leaving a trail of gore in its wake.

Whatever it had been that had got the better of him, it was now too late to worry about.

Davis had tried to keep pace with

Talbot. He had managed to do so until his fingers were pulling on spent triggers. Suddenly he realized that his Colts were empty. He holstered them and pulled the reins from his teeth.

He spurred even harder.

Somewhere beyond the wall of gun-smoke and swirling dust the remaining Apaches were still firing their rifles. Yellow flashes came out of the turbid mist and whizzed by him. Frantically trying to find a route out of the madness he had ridden into, Davis swung his horse to his right and dug both spurs into the creature's already bleeding flesh.

But as Davis galloped through the choking dust he realized that he had made the wrong choice of direction. Suddenly they were there ahead of him, kneeling between their ponies.

He could actually see the whites of the Apaches' eyes. Luckily for Davis the remaining Indians were as shocked and stunned as he was. He dragged the reins back and spurred again. His horse leapt over them before they could take aim.

Looking over his shoulder before the dust enveloped them once more Davis saw one of them train the long carbine barrel straight at him. Dragging his reins hard to his right he managed to turn his mount to the side. Then he heard the deafening sound behind him.

It was like being kicked by a mule in the back.

Liam Davis felt his right boot come from its stirrup as the forceful impact punched into his back. Somehow he managed to steady himself long enough for his boot to find the stirrup again.

Fighting the agonizing pain that had torn him apart, Davis galloped on through the dust.

'Keep riding, Liam boy!' Smith yelled out from the cover of his dead horse as Davis's mount headed toward him.

'Frank?' Davis blinked hard. Yet his eyes did not seem to work. It was like looking through a waterfall. He coughed and saw blood cover the mane of his still galloping horse.

'I'm hit, Frank!' Davis yelled out as he drew close to where Smith was waiting behind his fallen mount.

Smith did not reply. The outlaw just rose, stepped on top of his injured mount and threw himself at the passing horse.

Frank Smith grabbed Davis's saddle horn, swung his body and landed on the cantle behind his cohort. He reached around his wounded pal and then spurred as hard as he could.

With Apache bullets seeking them out, the horse thundered into another cloud of dust and gunsmoke. Smith did not stop his spurs from cutting into the flesh of Davis's animal until they had ridden out of range.

But the battle was not over behind them. With deadly precision Tate Talbot cocked the hammer of his .45 and squeezed its trigger until all six of the Colt's bullets had been discharged. Only then did he release the reins of Will Henry's mount and drag back on his own reins. He stopped his horse, dived for cover and then switched his empty .45 for its loaded twin.

He blasted six more shots to where he knew the Indians had to be, then lay as flat as he could. Bullets passed within a few inches above him.

The air was thick. Acrid smoke from the barrels of every weapon clouded the area as the remaining braves blasted their rifles in hope of hitting their elusive prey.

Talbot had not lived as long as he wanted to just yet. He would not give in easily. The sheriff of Senora rolled over and over into the dense churned-up dust cloud just as he heard the pitiful sound of his horse as it was riddled with bullets.

The animal staggered after its master and then fell heavily beside him. Talbot crawled to it and lay in the river of blood which ran from its wounds and shook the spent shells from his gun. The man who had always prided himself on his nerve found that he was fumbling with the bullets from his gunbelt as he listened to the rifle fire behind the stricken horse.

After managing to reload both his weapons, Talbot spun round in a kneeling position and crouched behind the saddle of his groaning animal. He holstered one and cocked the hammer of the other until it fully locked into position. He took a deep breath. He swallowed hard and forced himself to wait.

For what seemed like an eternity Tate Talbot bided his time as he listened intently to the rifle shots coming from where he had last seen the fearsome Apaches.

There was only one rifle being fired now, he told himself.

He looked all around him. Again he swallowed hard. Was he the only one of his gang still alive? The question burned into his mind like a branding-iron.

Talbot started to muster every ounce of his nerve and strength as he listened to the solitary rifle being cocked and fired. He raised his head above the saddle and squinted into the smoke and dust.

Talbot could see the white flashes as the surviving Indian's carbine fired one bullet after another.

The Apache was low.

Talbot lifted his arm over the saddle and aimed his readied weapon. He closed one eye and tried to estimate where he should send his deathly bullet.

Another flash came through the smoke.

Talbot squeezed his trigger.

There was no mistaking the sound of a man who had been hit dead centre by a .45 shell. Talbot drew his hammer back again and rose from the bloody sand. His gun barrel remained aimed at exactly the same spot. He was about to walk when he saw the Apache coming at him as the dust and smoke swirled away from the mortally wounded man who still held on to his rifle.

Again Talbot fired.

Again his aim was true.

The Indian was lifted off the sand and thrown backwards.

Talbot started to breathe again.

He staggered on and stared down at the Indian. He looked young. Real young, Talbot thought. Too damn young.

Step after step the outlaw leader continued until he reached the place which had been hidden from him for most of the brutal battle. There was blood everywhere. The blood of men and animals alike mixed and stained the sand he strode across.

Both his guns were drawn now.

His eyes darted from one body to the next. Even though it was obvious that all these painted men were dead, Talbot still feared them. Feared that they might leap to their feet and continue their fight.

Even death could not diminish their inherited magnificence.

Only when satisfied that they were truly dead did Talbot raise his eyes and look at the few ponies which had somehow managed to elude his bullets. The rest of the ponies were either dead or dying.

Talbot moved slowly through the dead men and animals and managed to grab the rope reins of the nearest pony. He pulled it towards him and ran a gloved hand down its nose.

There was no way that he would be able to put a saddle on the back of this creature, he told himself. He picked up a large water bag made from the innards of some unknown animal and hung it over the shoulders of the skittish pony.

Tate Talbot threw himself on to the back of the pony.

He rode away from the red sand.

12

Navajo Nate Willows was a man who had seen many things in his forty-nine years. Most of those things had been bad. The sickening sight which met him as the sun hung low in the afternoon sky was no better. In fact it was probably a lot worse. Death in the blistering heat of a desert beneath a remorseless sun had an aroma about it which travelled miles away from its core. It was a scent that filled the nostrils of animals and men alike. Once inhaled it could never be shaken loose or forgotten.

Willows had been an army scout for more than a quarter of his life. Before that he had lived with the Indians with whose tribal name he had been branded. He had been a fur-trapper in what was once simply known as Indian Territory. He had lived and traded with white and red men alike and knew at least half of the tribes which once flourished from Canada down to Mexico. But that had been a long time ago. A time before the greed of a few destroyed the lives of the many.

Willows had learned to speak the dialects of many of the Indians who had once freely frequented the vast uncharted lands. He was also an expert at talking with his hands to the many Plains tribes who had traded with him.

For years he had lived in peace and then he had become a scout for an army he knew would one day destroy the last remnants of a life he had once thought would last for ever. Yet Navajo Nate was paid well enough to keep him in chewing tobacco and hard liquor. Neither of which could compensate for the things he had witnessed since his return to so-called civilization. The sight before his sand-bruised eyes made his heart heavy.

He stopped his horse and sat silently. Even the seasoned army scout had never seen quite as much pointless carnage as this in such a small area. The dying rays of the sun had turned the sky red but it was no match for the red he saw upon the once white sand.

Willows tapped his boots against the sides of his mount and started to move forward. He rode between the bodies of the outlaws and the Apache warriors. Then he steered his horse around the dead and wounded ponies and horses. Of all the animals within this small desert hollow only two black-and-white ponies remained unscathed.

The moans of some of the horses chilled Willows to the bone.

His first instinct was to draw his gun and finish the wounded animals off but he had counted only about ten Apache bodies lying in the sand. Willows knew that there were meant to be as many again in the war party he had trailed from the reservation near Fort Myers.

If they were not here, where were they?

Would they return?

If they did he knew it would be the finish of him.

Navajo Nate hauled rein.

He turned the horse beneath him around and stared in disbelief at the sight and sounds. A million flies had already reached this place and were feasting. He saw a shadow trace across the sand and looked up. Now vultures were circling as they too inhaled the acrid stench of death as it rose on the highest of warm thermals.

Willows had heard the echoes of the brutal battle from more than ten miles back as he had doggedly tracked the twenty runaway Apaches. He had meant to turn and ride back to the column of cavalry but the sound of battle had lured him on.

Willows was like the flies which now buzzed over the corpses of men and beasts. He had been brought here by a power he did not understand. His hand vainly brushed the flies from his whiskered features.

The scout glanced around him.

Then he saw the twisted body of Will Henry. He turned his horse and allowed it to trot across the stained sand. He dropped from his saddle and closed the distance between himself and the broken corpse. Willows gritted his teeth and rubbed his neck.

He had seen death more times than he could recall but he still could not get used to it. It frightened him how something that was alive one moment could turn into this the next.

Even though the death had come only hours earlier the desert heat had caused the body to start stiffening and to stink worse than a dozen outhouses. He turned away and then saw what was left of Ken Davis. Willows walked to it with the reins of his horse gripped firmly in his left hand as his right wrist rested on the grip of his holstered gun. Flies were feasting on this body as well.

The veteran scout looked at the boot still in the stirrup and the saddle with its broken cinch strap a few yards away. His eyes glanced at the trail of gore left in the sand where the body had been dragged from the top of the high dune to his left. The horse had made it a few dozen yards further than its master but it had also fallen victim to the bullets of the young Apaches. Willows rubbed his face as if trying to rid his nostrils of the sickening smell, then he noticed something curious.

He looked around him and counted the dead saddle-horses which lay on the sand. There were four of them and yet only two bodies of white men. The scout bit his lip. He glanced all around the site of death and satisfied himself that there were no other bodies to be seen or found.

But where were the two other riders?

Then he remembered the ten or so other Apaches he knew had been with the dead ones who littered the sand. They might return, he told himself. He did not want to be here when they did.

Navajo Nate shook his head and turned to his horse.

He had seen enough.

The scout reached up and held on to his saddle horn before putting his left boot into his stirrup and mounting. The horse was skittish. The smell of death was everywhere and the animal wanted to put distance between them and the rotting bodies.

Willows flicked his reins across the back of his horse. It started to trot through the butchery. The scout knew that there should have been more Apaches than the ones which surrounded him.

His keen eyes searched the area and then he saw the tracks which led up into the place where the mesas started.

He was torn.

Every sinew in his aching body wanted to follow the trail and see where it led. That was what he was being paid to do. But he also knew that far behind him Captain Forbes and his men would be waiting. He sighed heavily and wondered why the white men lying here had fought with the Indians. Or maybe the Apaches had started it. Either way none of these dead folks had won the deadly encounter.

The army scout stood in his stirrups and whipped his long leathers across the shoulders of his mount.

The horse did not require much encouragement to get it galloping away from this place of death.

Navajo Nate rode hard.

He knew that he would return here. But the next time he would not be alone. The next time he would have eighteen cavalrymen with him.

The scout balanced in his stirrups and let his mount find its own pace. It did.

13

The sun had already fallen behind the golden-coloured mountains and darkness was spreading like a cancer throughout the strange uncharted land. With the darkness came a precarious descent into a place none of the young horsemen knew. To their right side rose a rugged jagged wall of untamed boulders whilst to their left was a drop of several hundred feet and certain death.

Yet they were unafraid. For fear was the one thing no Apache brave would ever acknowledge. It was an unknown emotion which served no purpose. There were only eight of the Apaches remaining now. They had heard the guns blazing behind them but by then they had already started down into the deep canyon which fringed the place where their dead were buried. A place which they knew the half-dozen braves from the unknown tribe and the young white man had defiled by entering. Although they could not enter the place where they cast the bodies of their dead they could try and find the point at which the intruders would make their getaway.

The steep rocky trail was narrow and only just capable of allowing the unshod ponies to negotiate it in single file. It was impossible for any of the war party to turn their mounts without falling into the perilous depths.

Against their better judgement the eight Apaches had to continue on down the steep trail carved by nature over countless generations, even though they wanted to return to the rest of their braves and discover what had happened back on the desert sand. But they would have to reach the bottom of the deep canyon before they could even think of returning.

Yet each of them silently knew that once they found the floor of the canyon they would probably have a new battle to win. For they had to punish those who had broken their taboos.

It was their law.

Shadows crept across the rocks, becoming blacker with every passing second. The riders gripped their ponies with powerful legs and leaned back. Even the ponies were anxious as they carefully put one hoof before another. This was a dangerous journey in daylight. At night it would verge on suicidal. Yet they continued.

Only mules could have navigated this trail easily. But mustangs were not mules. As darkness grew all around them the Indians continued fearlessly to urge their mounts on.

The lead rider was known as Nazimo. Some said he was the son of Geronimo but that was a distinction that all young defiant Apache bucks claimed. He had the spirit and courage of the great Apache leader even if he were not his son.

Nazimo had only one ambition. To

die like a man and not simply exist like a woman. Barely nineteen but with the eagle feathers to prove his manhood he had been the one to persuade his fellow young Apaches to leave the reservation and return to the place where he knew their tribe had once ruled.

So far half his followers had perished in the unforgiving desert. Nazimo greeted the stars with a mere glance and continued to lead the eight braves down into the darkness. If he knew that his fate was already written in those sparkling stars, he did not show it.

★　★　★

Hal Harper led his horse behind the five Indians who in turn guided their heavily laden ponies. They had travelled for nearly two miles away from the high-walled Apache graveyard into a labyrinth of cave tunnels. The open sky had disappeared from view shortly after they had begun their long trek and was now replaced by unyielding rock, which hung ominously above their heads.

The sand was still soft underfoot and slowed their progress as they all trailed Talka, who had travelled this way many times over the years. The Indian seemed to know every twist and turn of the maze of natural tunnels.

Harper remained at the back of the group and kept his eyes fixed on the pony just ahead of him, which was carrying the body of Talka's brother across its back.

The air was damp inside the caves. Yet, to Harper's surprise, there was light here. Strange growths upon the surfaces of the rocky walls all around them somehow glowed. A green eerie light filled the long tunnels just enough to allow those who walked through them the ability to see where they were.

Harper had never imagined anything like this before. It just seemed impossible that simple mosslike growths could give off any form of illumination at all.

As they reached the end of yet

another tunnel it appeared that they had walked into an enormous room. But this was no mere room. It was a cavernous void created over millions of years. Harper gasped and looked all around, then his eyes gazed upward. A high ceiling of jagged rock stretched across the entire area. They all paused. A few holes more than a hundred feet from the rocky floor allowed brief beams of moonlight to trace down into the huge cave. Then Harper saw something else high above. It appeared to be smoke trailing and using the holes to escape. Harper rubbed his eyes and then looked at the men who surrounded him. His mind raced and tried to work out the puzzle. It could not be smoke, he told himself. Smoke would require fire and this was just a damp cave. A damn big damp cave but just a damp cave all the same.

Harper stopped and pushed his battered hat off his head. He felt its drawstring touch his throat as the hat fell on to the back of his shirt. He looked harder at the braves. It was clear that they had all seen this place before.

'What wrong, Hal?' Talka asked, moving closer to the awestruck White Eyes drifter.

Harper had no words. He just gestured at the cave. It was far bigger than anything they had walked through since leaving the graveyard far behind them. Shafts of lights danced down stalactites of salty stone which hung from the highest point of the cave roof as water constantly dripped. Similar formations rose up from the very floor of the cave as if trying to reach their lofty brothers. It was a sight which astounded Harper.

'This cave is good!' Talka told the young drifter. 'This safe place for my people to rest and eat!'

Harper sighed. 'I ain't never seen the like before!'

Talka nodded and curled his finger. 'Come! Talka show you magic!'

'Magic?' Harper repeated the word and then followed the Indian. They walked among the eerie forest of stone until they reached something even more amazing to the eyes of the younger man. Now he knew that he had not imagined the smoke he had seen curling up around the top of the cave.

'I don't believe it!' Harper said.

Near the furthest wall of the cave, hidden by the many tall stone formations, a fire burned in a natural pit. Its flames licked up in an ever-changing pattern. It was warm and the youngster drew closer to it, felt its heat warm his aching bones.

'Fire never go away!' Talka told him.

Harper breathed in. It had the smell of a coal-oil lantern. He leaned closer and stared into the flames.

'Must be oil,' he said. 'Oil coming up from the bowels of Hell itself, I reckon!'

Talka nodded. 'Come from mother earth to warm us and let us cook our food, Hal. We come this way many times. It safe down here away from sun. Good place.'

Harper heard the rest of the small

band of Indians as they reached their leader with their horses in tow. Talka said something to the men and again they all silently obeyed his commands. Each went about his business with almost military precision.

One of the Indians pulled a deer from the back of his pony and placed it close to where the flames danced. He drew a long, wide-bladed knife from his beaded belt and began expertly to cut off one of the animal's already skinned legs. No city butcher could have done the job so neatly, Harper reckoned.

The Indian rested the meat in the flames and then returned the remains of the carcass to the back of his pony. Within seconds the savoury aroma of roasting meat filled Harper's nostrils.

'We eat when meat cooked, Hal,' Talka said.

'I sure could use me some meat to fill up my guts,' said Harper with a smile. 'My stomach's bin talking to me a whole heap for the last couple of hours, Talka.'

'I hear angry noises,' Talka nodded wryly.

'We gonna carry on after we eat?'

'No, we make camp here,' Talka said and clapped his hands. The sound echoed all around them. The rest of his small band started to prepare for their stay.

'I sure hope there ain't no man-eating critters in these caves,' Harper said, looking around nervously. 'I'd sure hate to end up as supper for a mountain lion.'

'Fire keep them away,' the Indian assured him. 'Lion no like fire. We will eat and drink and sleep. New day come many hours from now. Ponies need rest.'

Harper reached beneath the belly of his horse and started to undo his cinch straps. He pulled the saddle from the horse's back and laid it down on the ground. He then removed the bridle from the horse's head and patted the animal.

'We will water all horses soon,' Talka

said with a sigh as he sat down on the warm ground.

A high-pitched sound came from the other side of the cave. Harper stopped and stared. He knelt and drew his gun.

'What was that, Talka? Did ya hear it?'

'Bats, brave Hal. Just little bats.' Talka smiled. 'They no eat you.'

★　★　★

Darkness had brought a cold chill to the high rocks overlooking the arid desert and canyons. Yet Tate Talbot knew that he dare not light a fire. He had already survived one battle with Apaches and knew that he did not have the stomach for another. A stiff breeze cut through the gaps in the jagged rocks where he had secreted himself and the pony. He found half a cigar, placed it between his teeth and started to chew on it. Even the thought of striking a match made him uneasy. A naked flame against the backdrop of a black sky might bring a bullet.

Talbot was restless as well as cold. He wondered what his next move ought to be but found no answers in his weary mind. It had all gone wrong. His greed had brought him to within a whisker of death and he knew it. His plan of claiming the bounty on his own head now seemed to be ridiculous. If only he had been able to shoot the young stranger in the Senora cantina as he had wanted to do things would have been so very different.

The chase had been costly. Too damn costly.

Reluctantly Talbot knew that the young drifter was by now long gone. Now there was no way that he could execute his devious plan. Whoever that stranger had been, he was now safe. Unlike Talbot himself.

Again Talbot glanced up at the stars and moon above him. Everything around him was bathed in a mixture of black shadow and a grey illumination. He kept close to a rock and held on to the crude rope rein of the pony. Yet the wind seemed to find him however much he attempted to elude its bone-cutting fury.

He stared at the pony and wished it had been his own horse. His own horse had had plenty of grub in its saddlebags and water in its canteens.

His eyes narrowed. Down there a few miles away lay provisions and water, he told himself. Why had he left it there? Had the brutal encounter with the Apaches robbed him of his sanity as well as his gang?

Was it all down to fear? Had he been so scared that he had simply run away without giving any thought to what he might do when hunger and thirst overwhelmed him?

His throat felt as though a bowie knife had slit it from ear to ear. He was dry and hungry. His guts churned in protest at not being supplied with grub for more than half a day.

A mixture of anger and nervousness made Talbot pull his guns from their holsters and check them.

Then he remembered that he had already checked them at least twenty times since he had ridden up into this high remote sanctuary.

They were fully loaded and he had a few shells left on his gunbelt. He shook his head, slid both weapons back into their leather homes on his hips and rubbed his hands together. Even his gloves could not stop the cold which seemed constantly to be eating into his flesh and bones.

How could a place that could bake a man dry in the hours of daylight change so much? He was freezing to death up on the side of this rockface. Talbot got on to one knee and surveyed the land below him. The moonlight lit up enough of it for him to see if there were any other Apaches wandering around looking for a prime scalp to add to their war lances.

For more than ten minutes he vainly kept up his vigil. He watched a few deer running across the dunes and then to his surprise he saw dust drifting up from beyond the boulders at the foot of the towering rock beneath which he was perched.

Dust could mean that death was seeking him out once more.

Talbot moved to a flat overhang. He lay across it and carefully crawled close to its edge. It was a sheer drop of a couple of hundred feet but Talbot was too tired to be scared. He leaned over and squinted hard.

More dust filtered up and drifted out from far below his high vantage point.

He was certain that something or someone was moving far below: moving close to where he had started his own ascent to the place where he now lay.

But who or what was down there?

It was impossible to see.

All he knew for certain was that it was not the night breeze which was kicking up the dust. Something living was moving down there just beyond his range of vision. A bead of sweat defied his chilled flesh and ran down his face.

Cautiously Talbot eased himself back until he was on firm ground again, then he inhaled deeply. Could it be more hostiles? Could the rest of the tribe have found their dead and tracked him to this place? If so, how long would it be before they started up the rockface in search of him?

This was no place to defend yourself against an attack.

Talbot tied the rope reins around his left boot, found a match and struck it with his thumbnail. He cupped the flame and put it to the end of the cigar in his mouth. He sucked in the smoke and blew out the match. He no longer feared them seeing him.

'C'mon,' he whispered angrily and pulled out his guns again. 'I'm ready for ya. I'll kill all of ya.'

Then he heard a sound.

It was hoofs on rocks.

A horse.

No horse would come up here of its

own choice. Only a horse with a rider on its back would be loco enough to do that. Just as he had done.

He cocked the hammers of his guns and waited.

14

It was a blood-curdling noise which echoed in the cold night air all around the rocks which jutted up from the desert floor. The sound of hoofs on the twisting trail up to where Tate Talbot waited grew ever louder. The outlaw who wore the tin star upon his chest grew more and more anxious. His gloved hands clutched on to his pair of cocked .45s as sweat traced down his features. With every pounding beat of his heart the sound increased. One hoof after another in an almost tormenting fashion. Talbot moved his weight from one leg to the other. He knew that he could have remained on the flat rock which hung over the mountainous precipice and watched the horseman from a spot that could have allowed him to pick the rider off. But he had chosen to remain up against the moonlit rockface with both his weapons drawn and readied.

He knew that he had chosen the wrong option.

From where he was secreted he could not see who was heading up to where he hid. His eyes darted back and forth from beneath the brim of his hat and focused across at the rocks at the top of the steep stony trail.

He watched, as all frightened creatures watch for the first sign of danger to rear its ugly head.

Starved of sleep, food and water, Talbot's mind raced.

Was it another Apache? Maybe it was more than one. Did Indians fight at night?

Talbot knew that he had made no efforts to hide the tracks of the pony when he had fled the bloody battle scene. Anyone with half an eye could have trailed him to this place. His heart began to race.

He tried to swallow but his dry throat refused to obey. He wanted to cough but again fear prevented it. Slowly he began to crouch down. He knew that he was a big target even to someone who was not the best of shots. Talbot fell on to one knee and then the other. Again his eyes searched the area for something to use as cover. But there were no boulders up here close to the top of the towering rock formation. Talbot realized that when the shooting started it would probably be the end of him.

He started to breath heavily.

Talbot had been an outlaw for most of his grown days and had faced many men wielding knives, guns and rifles without even flinching, but this was quite different.

He was scared.

Scared of the unknown horseman who continued to force his mount ever upward towards him. Talbot had lost all of his men due to his own greed and suddenly realized that for the first time since he had ridden on the wrong side of the law, he was entirely alone.

He had always been part of a gang.

For the first part of his infamous career he had been one of the riders. Then he had formed his own gang. The men who had followed his lead had changed over the years as one by one they had been killed. But there had never been any problem finding men willing and able to replace those he had lost.

But now he was alone.

Quite alone.

The sweat was now flowing down his face. He screwed up his eyes and kept them homed in on the top of the trail where his ears told him that the rider would soon appear. Seconds seemed to last a lifetime as he waited.

Then he saw him.

The moon was behind the mounted figure. All he could see was a black shape astride an even blacker horse. Talbot rose fast and raised his guns until his arms were fully outstretched.

'Haul rein, ya bastard!' Talbot snarled.

The rider drew his reins up to his chest. The horse stopped and snorted. Talbot moved closer. This was no

Apache, he silently told himself. This was a white man.

'Who are ya?' Talbot growled even louder.

'Howdy, Tate,' the rider's voice said.

Talbot's jaw dropped. 'Frank?'

'Who the hell was ya expecting, Tate?' Smith chuckled.

Talbot dropped his guns into his holsters and raised a hand to shield his eyes from the moon over the rider's shoulder. He looked at the face and wished it had been another one of his gang members. Anyone except Frank Smith.

'I thought ya was dead. I thought ya all was dead.'

Frank Smith looped his leg over the neck of his mount and slid from his saddle. He looked down at the eerie landscape stretched out far below them before returning his gaze to the sweating man beside him.

'I nearly was, Tate,' Smith answered. 'They back-shot Liam and I had to dump his dead carcass a few miles from here. Man, them Injuns sure is ornery, ain't they?'

'So we're the only ones left?' Talbot said. 'Damn it all!'

'Yep.' Smith pulled his canteen from the saddle horn and handed it to Talbot. 'Just you and me.'

Talbot grabbed the canteen, unscrewed its stopper and took two long swallows. He sighed and then handed it back to Smith who returned it to the saddle.

Even the moonlight could not hide the expression carved into Smith's face. It was the look of an ambitious man.

'What ya looking at?' Talbot snapped.

'I'm looking at you, Tate,' Smith snapped back. 'Ya looks like a man that's beat. I ain't beat. I'm still willing to carry on and finish the job we come out here to do. I wanna catch that Casey critter and claim that reward money.'

Tate Talbot looked at the ground. 'No, we gotta head back to Senora, Frank. It's over.'

'Over?' Smith grabbed the shirt collar

of his companion. 'Ya willing to kiss twenty thousand dollars goodbye? Just 'coz we lost a few men?'

Talbot pulled Smith's hands away. 'It's over I tell ya. That critter is miles away from here by now.'

Smith suddenly clenched both his fists and threw a left to Talbot's belly. When that brought the winded man's head down Smith smashed his right across the side of Talbot's jaw. The older man fell to the ground.

'I'm leading this party from here on in,' Smith said. 'Ya better savvy that darn fast or I'll kill you as well.'

Talbot raised his head. Blood trickled from the corner of his mouth. 'But that young drifter ain't really Diamond Bob Casey, Frank. I made that up.'

Smith hauled the bigger man back to his feet. He shook him hard and glared into his eyes.

'What?' he yelled.

'I just had me this idea that I could kill someone that nobody knew and say it was Casey. The reward money would

157

have to be paid.' Talbot coughed. 'Don't ya get it? It was all a big trick to claim the bounty.'

Smith released his grip. He turned and stared out at the strange landscape again. For a few moments he remained silent. Then he glanced at Talbot again, this time with even more fury in his eyes.

'It don't matter none. We're still going to kill that varmint, Tate. That's too much money to turn our backs on.'

Talbot wiped his mouth with his glove. He looked at his blood glisten in the moonlight. Then he nodded.

'OK,' he agreed.

'I reckon I know where he went,' Smith said. 'I found me some tracks that lead down into a canyon. Some Apaches went down there but I found me another set of tracks. The tracks of a shod horse. That's gotta be him. There ain't no other horse with shoes in this desert.'

'More Apaches?' Talbot said.

'Ya scared of a few Injuns, Tate?'

'Damn right!'

15

Dawn raced across the desert quickly. Within minutes the temperature had risen by ten degrees. The troop of cavalrymen had been led by the seasoned Navajo Nate Willows to the place where at least half the young Apache braves they had been charged with bringing back to the reservation lay festering in the stained desert sand. The smell was already sickening and the air was filled with excited flies. Not one corpse of either man or animal had escaped the onslaught of voracious insects. As the horsemen approached half-a-dozen vultures lifted off the sand and flew up into the sky.

They would circle until it was safe for them to return to their feasting. Every eye watched them as they floated around high above the small patrol of troopers.

Captain Eli Forbes raised his hand and stopped his powerful mount as his scout dropped down from his horse and began his inspection of the dead. Forbes dismounted and handed his reins to his sergeant. The officer followed the scout to the nearest of the saddle horses. The stench was almost unbearable and yet the scout seemed immune to the horrific odour.

Navajo Nate Willows was scratching his head with one hand whilst the other fended off the attention of the flies with broad sweeps.

Forbes edged closer. 'You said earlier, when you returned to the troop, that there were too many saddle horses for the number of bodies of white men, Navajo.'

'Sure enough,' Willows nodded.

'Are you certain?' Forbes said, holding a white-gloved hand in front of his mouth.

Willows nodded and quickly pointed around them. 'Yep. We're short of some dead folks, I reckon.'

Forbes narrowed his eyes against the flies. 'You said that there are four horses and only two bodies?'

'Yep.'

'Then at least two men escaped this fight,' Forbes said thoughtfully. 'I wonder who they were and where they went?'

'They headed yonder!' The scout waved his hand towards where the high mesas could be seen far beyond dunes.

'Devil's Elbow?' Forbes suggested.

'That's what they called the place.'

'The ancestral home of the Apache.'

'Not all of them, Captain.' Willows glanced briefly at the man in dust-caked blue. 'Just the ones young Nazimo is kin to.'

Eli Forbes could not stand the stench any longer. He turned away and coughed.

Willows began to walk again. With every step his knowing eyes lit upon something new. Something which he had not noticed on his previous visit to this macabre battle ground. The military officer walked at the side of his scout. He had been on many battle-fields after the gunsmoke ceased but death was something which he had never been able to get used to.

He paused as he noticed the scout leaning over the bodies of the dead braves. He watched as the scout turned each of the young bodies over and looked hard into their already rotting features.

'What of Nazimo?' Forbes asked.

Navajo Nate turned and looked beneath bushy eyebrows at the captain. 'He ain't here.'

Forbes stepped closer. 'Are you sure, Navajo?'

Willows nodded firmly. 'I know that hot-head real well, Captain. He ain't here.'

Forbes turned away from the pile of bodies and tried to rid his nostrils of the acrid stench. It was impossible. He had never seen the Apache brave known as Nazimo but had heard a lot about him. He was the most dangerous of them all. A man who had the spirit of an entire nation surging through his veins. No other Apache, apart from the famed Geronimo, could stir up his fellow braves quite as well as Nazimo.

Forbes sighed and returned his eyes to the scout. 'That's a shame, Navajo. Without Nazimo the rest of them would be easy to round up. Like headless chickens.'

Willows stepped over the buzzing sand and stood next to the captain. He knew the man was close to the end of his long career.

'I'd suggest we return back to Fort Myers if it weren't for the fact that Nazimo is still running loose, sir.'

Forbes punched one gloved fist into the palm of his other.

'We cannot quit without Nazimo, Navajo. Dead or alive I have to take him back to Fort Myers.'

'I knew ya would say that, Captain,' Willows said, nodding. 'I can lead ya on after that young troublemaker. His trail went up yonder.'

The tired cavalry officer looked to

where his scout was pointing. He could see the high golden-coloured mesas beyond the rolling sand dunes. He had never been in a land anything like this one and did not like it one bit. His eyes darted back to Willows.

'What's out there, Navajo? What can we expect?' he whispered. 'I have to consider the men. Can white men survive in that sort of terrain?'

'There's death out there, Captain! Sand and rocks and a whole bunch of things that can kill even more painfully than the worst Apache ya ever did meet.' Willows shuddered. 'I ain't travelled too far into that land. It kinda makes ya want to turn and ride away. That's what I did. I turned my old horse and rode away as fast as the poor critter could go.'

'That bad?'

'Worse.'

The cavalry officer looked to Coogan. 'Get the men to round up all the rifles and rifle rounds they can find, Coogan.'

The sergeant saluted and pointed at

three of the mounted men.

'Ya heard the captain. Round up all the weapons!'

The enlisted men did as ordered and reluctantly approached the decaying bodies.

Forbes patted the scout's shoulder and walked back across the sand to his horse. He took up the reins and stepped into his stirrup. As he settled down on his saddle he watched as the scout threw himself up on to his own mount and gathered up his reins.

'Are we gonna carry on, sir?' Sergeant Coogan asked.

'The job has yet to be finished, Coogan,' Forbes replied.

Sergeant Coogan watched his superior officer pull out a map from a saddlebag and carefully unfold it. His eyes went from the paper to the scout, who was already cutting a trail between the bodies of the animals and men who were scattered before them.

'Where's Willows headed, sir?' Coogan asked as his men completed their task and piled the rifles on the backs of their pack animals.

Forbes tapped his spurs against the side of his horse and started to follow Willows. 'Navajo Nate is taking us into Devil's Elbow. The place which, they say, these Apaches regard as their home.'

'But what do we know about Devil's Elbow, sir?' Coogan asked. He mounted, waved an arm and started the troop after Forbes and the scout.

'See for yourself.' Captain Forbes turned and handed the map to Coogan as the burly rider drew level. Coogan stared at the map. Apart from the name there was nothing else upon its printed surface.

'But, Captain,' Coogan said fearfully, 'it ain't got nothing printed on it that we can use. No trail or river markings or anything. We ain't got no idea what's out there sir.'

Forbes nodded.

'We know one thing, Coogan. Nazimo and what's left of his war party are out there. And we're going to get them.'

The cavalrymen rode on through the sand beneath the rising sun, following the tracks left by the scout's horse.

Even before the dust from their horses' hoofs settled the vultures came floating down and resumed their fight over the rich pickings.

16

The shafts of sunlight had stretched down from the small holes far above in the ceiling of the cave. Talka had been first to awaken. Anyone who knew him would have doubted that he had even slept at all. His was the role of leader. It was a duty he had not chosen for himself but one which he refused to relinquish. He led and he tried to protect those who looked to him as their chief. For most of his adult life Talka had led small hunting parties from his distant homeland to the desert that had once been occupied by Apaches. Yet this was probably going to be the last time the dry arid desert would be visited by the tribe with no name.

Once there had been plentiful game amid the dunes. Enough for both Apaches and his own tribe. But now most of the game was gone, like the buffalo further north. Talka knew that he would have to find another hunting ground.

After watering the horses Talka had roused the other braves silently and then turned his attention to the young white man they had saved from the merciless desert a couple of days earlier.

Hal Harper felt the hand on his shoulder and jumped up from his bedroll beside the flames of the strange eternal fire. He blinked hard and then focused on the amused face of Talka.

He sighed heavily.

'Talka.'

'We ready to go now, White Eyes Hal.' The brave stood and helped Harper up from the sand. The light of the flames danced across both men as they moved to their mounts.

Harper tossed the blanket across the back of his horse and patted it down firmly. He then bent down and sleepily lifted the hefty saddle up. He threw the saddle over the blanket and then lifted the left stirrup up and hooked it over the saddle horn.

Talka and the other Indians watched as the young man reached under the belly of the horse and pulled both the cinch straps in turn towards him. They were fascinated by how complicated it was for a white man to ready his mount.

Harper saw the men beside him and glanced at them. 'What ya looking at?'

Talka pointed at the saddle. 'White Eyes Hal work very hard to get pony ready. We only need blanket. Why Hal and other white men need all that?'

Harper raised his eyebrows. It was a good question and one he did not have an answer for. But he had to say something to the men who had looked after him as if he were one of them.

'White folks tend to fall off their horses a lot more than his red brothers, Talka. We needs all this stuff just to stay on the backs of our animals.'

Talka nodded and turned. He raised

a hand and waved it at his followers. Within seconds they had all thrown themselves on the backs of their ponies. Harper held on to his saddle horn and thrust his left boot into the stirrup. He mounted slowly beside the waiting riders.

'We go.' Talka pointed ahead.

The ponies led the way with Harper at the rear of their small band as before. Again Talka led them expertly through the maze of strange stone columns which seemed to have grown out of the very cave floor itself. Then he guided those who trailed him into yet another long cave tunnel.

This time it was dark. There was no light from anywhere and yet the lead rider seemed to be able to navigate the twists and turns without any problem at all. The other braves stayed close and Harper was forced to use his ears to listen to where the horse ahead of him was moving in order to steer his own horse without colliding with the tunnel walls.

For more than an hour the line of riders trailed after Talka until all of them could see the sunlight ahead of them. It was bright, almost blinding, yet Talka continued leading them with his hooded eyes seemingly immune to its brilliance. Harper knew that this was no ordinary man. There was a greatness about him which the young horseman had to admire.

At last the ponies and the solitary horse reached the cave mouth and the light. The ponies increased their pace and trotted out first, as if they wanted to shake the chill of the cave off their coats. The heat of the sun was felt immediately by them all.

Harper was last to leave the cave tunnel. He pulled his hat off his back by its drawstring and pulled its brim down to shield his eyes.

He looked all around. The buttes and the mesas rose like golden statues created by mythical giants. He had never seen anything like these rocks which surrounded them before. In his long journey to this secret place there had been nothing to compare with the sheer grandeur of it.

But his awe was short-lived.

Suddenly, without warning, rifles opened up from far above them. The entire canyon shook with the deafening sound of bullets as they twisted down and bounced off the boulders to either side.

Talka swung his terrified pony around and pointed up at the plumes of deadly gunsmoke.

He yelled out his warning loud and clear.

'Apaches!'

17

There might have only been eight Apaches on the rocks but their prowess with the repeating rifles made it seem as though an entire battalion had suddenly unleashed its venomous fury on the Indians and Harper below. The morning air was filled with gunsmoke as deafening volleys of rifle fire sought out the handful of riders. Bullets tore down into the heat haze from both sides. Lead ricocheted off the rockfaces around them, showering debris over the horsemen. Until the moment that the shooting started Harper had not realized that the Indians he rode with did not have any firearms of their own. Their entire arsenal consisted of nothing more than simple bows and arrows.

The young horseman drew and started to return fire as he saw one of the closest braves hit by well-aimed shots. His back exploded in a mess of scarlet gore. After twisting in the air for a few seconds the Indian fell from his pony and landed just ahead of Harper's own mount.

Harper dragged rein and spun his animal around. Looking upward he saw the rifle barrels which jutted from above the golden-coloured rocks. He took aim and fanned the hammer of his six-shooter to give Talka and the remaining Indians a chance to get their bows and arrows into action. Within seconds the Indians around him started to send their lethal arrows up at their attackers.

The small canyon was filled with choking debris as bullets tore into the rockface.

Harper spurred and rode towards Talka just as the Indian leader sent one of his deadly projectiles up into the rocks far above them. An Apache screamed out as the arrow sank into his chest. The warrior tumbled and fell from the rocks. A plume of dust rose up from the canyon floor as the body landed hard between two of the ponies.

The battle carried on regardless.

'We better get out of here, Talka!' Harper yelled as he shook spent brass casings from his smoking gun and quickly reloaded it with fresh bullets from his belt. 'They'll finish us all off if'n we don't!'

Talka did not speak.

There was no time for words.

He kept plucking arrows from a leather bag which hung from the neck of his pony, placing them on the bow and letting them fly towards the rifle smoke.

Some of the rest of his braves hastily plucked their dead comrade off the sand and placed the limp body over the back of the nervous pony. Only when they had achieved this courageous deed did Talka look at Harper.

'Now we go!' Talka shouted out loudly over the sound of the constant rifle shots.

The ponies thundered along the

dusty trail as the Apaches leapt down from their lofty perches, scrambling down the rocks towards their own hidden mounts. Some of Nazimo's men still managed to keep firing their carbines as they reached their ponies.

The chase was on.

★ ★ ★

Against his better judgement Tate Talbot had followed the route taken by Nazimo and his braves down the steep trail and he descended into the blazing-hot canyon with Smith a length behind him. The man who wore a star, but in reality was a wanted outlaw, knew that if he were to tell his companion that he was really the infamous Diamond Bob Casey he would end up as dead as those they had left behind them back on the desert sand.

Talbot knew that Smith had never actually liked playing second fiddle to him and if he even suspected the truth the outlaw would not think twice about

177

putting bullets into his back to claim the bounty.

Both riders had only just reached the floor of the rocky canyon when they had heard the sound of rifle fire ahead of them.

They steadied their mounts as the echoes of the bullets surrounded them. It had come as a surprise to them both. They wondered who, apart from the drifter whom they had trailed all the way from Senora, was out here in the unholy land?

Then Talbot started to think that his fear of there being even more Apaches out here in this cursed desert might be closer to the truth than he had imagined.

Talbot swung his lathered-up pony around and stared at Frank Smith. Smith's face had fear carved into it.

'What the hell was that, Tate?' Smith asked. He eased his horse closer to the Indian pony and stared along the canyon. 'Who would be shooting out there?'

Talbot had no answers. The firing continued.

'We ought to get out of here, Frank. Whoever it is that's doing all that shooting, it sure sounds like there's an awful lot of them.'

Smith gritted his teeth. He knew the older rider was right but he wanted to collect the bounty. He could almost smell the $20,000 Talbot had told him about.

'I ain't yella,' he snarled. 'I ain't the sort who turns and runs when the shootin' starts. Ya know that.'

'Sure I know that, Frank. But it ain't yella to light out when the odds are against ya, Frank.' Talbot spoke through dry, cracked lips. 'If we go back to Senora we can always find ourselves another drifter to kill and claim the reward money for. We don't need that varmint. What ya say?'

Furiously, Smith slapped the neck of his tired mount. He thought for a few moments and then reluctantly spun his horse around.

He had been about to agree, but then his eyes narrowed as they saw the line of troopers descending towards them. The cavalrymen were still a couple of hundred yards above them but the narrow trail meant that it was now impossible for them to get out of the hot canyon by the same way as they had entered it.

'Troopers!' Smith pointed a crooked finger. 'Look up there, Tate! A whole bunch of troopers!'

Talbot rode closer to his partner and raised a hand to cover his eyes from the blinding rays of the sun. His guts churned as he focused on the familiar figure of the officer who rode just behind the scout. Even at this distance Talbot could tell who the military officer was by the way he rode.

'Damn it all!' Talbot cursed out loud. 'Not him! For Christ's sake, not him!'

'What's wrong, Tate?' Smith asked.

'I know that damn officer up there, Frank,' Talbot admitted. 'I had me a run in with that critter about six or so years back. He ain't changed one bit.'

Smith held on to his reins tightly. 'Does he know ya a wanted outlaw?'

'Yep,' Talbot answered. 'Reckon he ain't ever likely to forget me or my face.'

'What ya do to him to make ya so memorable?'

'I killed his son.'

Smith looked around them. The high canyon walls were almost sheer. There was only one way they could go and that was in the same direction as the Apaches had taken hours earlier. He stared into the swirling heat haze which blurred the canyon. The gunfire still resounded.

'Then we better ride, Tate. We don't want no soldier boys to spoil our plans.'

Talbot pulled on his rope reins and again turned the pony around. It was impossible to tell what lay ahead but it had to be better than remaining where they were, to await the cavalrymen and their leader. Captain Eli Forbes was one man the outlaw did not want to tangle with again.

Both outlaws spurred and rode into the unknown depths of the canyon. The further they travelled the louder the rifle shots got.

Far above them Forbes lowered his field glasses and took a deep breath as he carefully steered his mount down the steep rocky trail after the scout. He had recognized Talbot instantly. Like the outlaw, the memory of the man was branded into his mind for eternity. Only death could erase it.

'Who were they, Captain?' Coogan asked from behind Forbes.

'One is an outlaw called Diamond Bob Casey, Sergeant,' Forbes replied.

'How'd ya know that, sir?'

'You never forget the faces of men you've vowed to kill, Coogan,' Forbes told him.

18

A few minutes had made the vital difference between life and death for Talka, Harper and the remaining Indians. Most had avoided the bullets of their bushwhackers, but not all. Now there were two bodies tied to the backs of ponies. Time had given them a good quarter-mile lead of their pursuers. The small hunting party and the lone rider had forced their mounts to reach break-neck speed before Nazimo and his half-dozen followers had managed to reach their own mounts.

Yet the Apaches were by far the more skilled horsemen of the two tribes and had soon managed to close down the distance between them. Every stride of the painted ponies had seen the Apaches get closer.

At full pace, Talka aimed his wide-eyed mount down into a draw.

The others trailed him. Then he spun his pony around and led them through a narrow split in the high wall of rock which was barely wider than their ponies. Talka had been here many times before and was using his knowledge to try to save them from the Apaches' fury. It did not work. The young Apaches were not so easily shaken off. They were like a lizard who, once it has closed its jaws on its victim, it could not release its grip.

Soon Talka and his small party were headed back out towards the middle of the canyon. Clouds of dust spewed up from the arid canyon ground as the ponies and saddle horse galloped across its dry surface. But the rifle bullets again started to seek them out. Each shot got closer.

The deafening noise as red-hot tapers of lead poison passed through the dust and bounced off the canyon walls around them was a chilling reminder that Nazimo wanted to punish and kill them all.

Knowing that they needed more speed from their mounts, the riders threw the heavy water bags off the shoulders of their ponies in an attempt to increase their pace. It worked. Suddenly the small muscular mustangs were able to lift their forelegs high off the ground as they drove across the unforgiving terrain.

Talka led his small band from one side of the canyon to the other. There stood rounded giant boulders left from a time when the entire region had been covered in ice. The boulders were as big as houses and dotted throughout the canyon. The leader of the tribe with no name used his arms to encourage his pony to find a pace that should have been impossible in the blazing heat. He rode along the canyon and negotiated its twists and turns with an expertise born of knowledge of a place he had visited many times.

It began to dawn on Talka that he would never reach his homeland if the Apaches managed to get any closer.

The Indian leader steered his pony in between the great rocks, knowing that they were the only cover he and the riders behind him had within the confines of the sun-bleached canyon. The others raced in the tracks of his unshod mount.

The dust grew thicker behind them as it was thrown up from the hoofs of their fleeing mounts. Yet the Apaches still fired their rifles even though they could not see their targets.

With hot lead cutting through the dust, Hal Harper spurred his powerful mount and drew level with Talka. He glanced at the face of the Indian. He had never seen anyone with so much determination before. This was a man who knew that the survival of not only himself but those who looked to him for guidance was at stake.

Talka could not afford to make any more mistakes. He had already lost two of his small hunting party and the odds were stacked against him.

They trailed the brave down through

a sandy draw, over a small hill of sand set between two boulders and into a forest of tall cactus and Joshua trees. Talka pointed to their right and slowly began to ease his pony towards a place which was dense with viciously spiked cactus.

Desperately trying to keep up with young but far more experienced Talka, Harper ate the choking dust and followed. As the animals ploughed through the gaps between the cactus and the Joshua trees Harper thought that if a man made one false move here, he could have been skinned alive by the vegetation. The smaller ponies made easier work of it than his bigger horse. Harper felt the sleeves being ripped from his arms as he vainly attempted to find a clear, safe trail between the forest of spikes.

Then, just as they cleared the last of the angry, flesh-slashing plants, Talka drew rein and turned his pony in an attempt to head into a small draw.

Another volley of bullets tore through

the wall of dust behind them. This time some of those bullets found their target.

Harper dragged his horse to a stop when he saw Talka slump over the neck of his pony. Without a thought for his own safety the young drifter spurred and forced his horse to leap across the rough ground until he was next to the chieftain. He dismounted quickly and rushed to the pony. Harper caught Talka before his bloodied body hit the ground.

The other braves rode close. They too ignored the bullets which kept on coming through the fog of dust. A pony was hit just as its master jumped clear. It fell on to the sand and kicked its legs out as life quickly drained from it.

'Go, White Eyes Hal!' Talka commanded as he was cradled in the arms of the youngster. 'Go! I Talka command it!'

Harper held on to the warrior as the others gathered around him. They all knelt beside their leader.

'Go!' Talka said weakly.

'I ain't going no place, Talka,' Harper gritted. 'Not without you, anyways.'

Suddenly the dust parted like the waves of the Red Sea. Seven Apache braves proudly rode through the dense barrier and encircled the kneeling men before them. Each rifle barrel was trained on them as Nazimo kicked the sides of his black-and-white pony and approached.

Harper looked up at the Apache.

'Howdy!' he said.

Nazimo raised his rifle above his head and gave out a chilling victory war cry. He then waved the carbine at his men and spat out a few words. The braves dropped down to the sand and moved towards their prisoners. Each had his finger balanced on his rifle trigger.

'You all die!' Nazimo said in broken English.

'Ya know somethin'? I'm damned if I really care!' Harper replied, holding the wounded Talka in his blood-covered arms.

Nazimo moved closer to the defiant Harper.

'You I will kill slow, white man.'

'Good,' Harper retorted. 'I ain't in no hurry.'

The young Apache warrior pushed the hand-guard of his carbine down. A spent casing was expelled before he drew it back up and cocked the rifle into action. His thumb pulled the trigger back. The sound of it clicking into position filled the desert air. Each of the braves huddled close and Harper and Talka looked at one another silently.

Then another sound filled the canyon beyond the cloud of swirling dust behind the Apaches. It was the sound of horses charging across the arid terrain. It echoed all around them.

Harper noticed Nazimo's eyes as they darted to his fellow braves. He turned and stared into the dust like a statue, waiting for it to clear.

Then it did and Nazimo could see the distant horsemen.

'Men and soldiers!' he exclaimed angrily.

Two of his fellow tribesmen moved closer to him.

'We must go!' one of them urged.

'Not before we kill those who have defiled our dead!' Nazimo spat his words out at the sand.

The Apache next to Nazimo raised his rifle and pointed its long barrel at the riders who were getting closer with every passing heartbeat.

'No time, Nazimo. Soldiers come for us.'

Nazimo grunted. 'We kill soldiers.'

19

The two outlaws whipped and spurred their mounts and rode deeper and deeper into the canyon towards the well-armed Indians whom they had yet to see. Both horsemen had looked over their shoulders several times and could not believe their eyes. The cavalrymen were now in hot pursuit of them. Neither man knew that Captain Eli Forbes had dismissed any thoughts of Nazimo and the other Apaches he had travelled so far to capture or kill. All the cavalry officer could think of now was the face he had seen through his field glasses. A face he had not been able to rid his nightmares of for over six years.

The face of Diamond Bob Casey was branded into his mind.

It had been the only thing to keep him out here in this arid land for so long. He could have retired three years earlier and returned East with a tidy pension, but that would have robbed him of the chance to find and kill Casey.

It was the only thing which had kept Forbes alive.

Now Forbes could actually see the rider ahead of him. A rider who was not having any joy controlling the bareback Indian pony beneath him.

The troop of eighteen cavalrymen and the scout were spread out wide as they thundered along the canyon after the pair of men they knew must be wanted outlaws.

The larger saddle horse that Frank Smith rode was now finding its long legs capable of far greater speed than the smaller Indian pony Talbot was riding. It started to draw ahead. But to ride ahead of a man like Talbot, or Diamond Bob Casey, was not the smartest thing to do.

At last Tate Talbot had his chance. He would take it.

The outlaw drew one of his deadly

.45s from its holster and aimed at the rider who was now two horse's lengths ahead of him.

He squeezed the trigger and watched Smith's back explode as the bullet found its mark. Smith released the grip of his reins, arched his back just as Talbot sent a second lethal shot into him.

The larger horse began to slow as the spurs were no longer being rammed into its flesh. Smith's body rotated atop the saddle for a few moments as Talbot forced the Indian pony to draw level.

Balancing astride the unsaddled pony, Talbot raised his right boot and placed it on the back of the galloping pony. He straightened his leg, rose and catapulted himself across the distance between them. He landed on to the horse just behind his lifeless companion.

Without a second thought, Talbot pushed Smith aside. The body fell and hit the ground hard and rolled across the sun-baked ground but Talbot did not see it. He grabbed the saddle horn, jumped on to the seat of the saddle and poked both boots into the stirrups. He gathered up the reins and whipped the mount's shoulders. The horse responded and vainly tried to ride away from the pain which kept on coming.

Sergeant Coogan looked across at the face of the cavalry captain who rode beside him.

'Did ya see that? He just killed his pal, sir!' the sergeant shouted out.

But Forbes just narrowed his eyes against the dust they were thundering into. He ignored Coogan's shout and pointed one of his white gauntlets ahead.

'Look, Coogan!'

Coogan screwed up his eyes to where Captain Forbes was pointing. Then, through the shimmering haze, he saw them.

The near-naked men painted for war were standing defiantly waiting for them to ride into range of their rifles. Coogan's head turned back to his superior officer.

'Nazimo!'

'To hell with Nazimo!' Forbes bellowed back. 'I've got other fish to fry!'

'What'll we do about those Injuns?' Coogan hollered.

But Forbes did not care about the Apache warriors. His thoughts were for one man only. He could see Talbot turning his horse and heading towards the golden-coloured buttes to their left. He quickly glanced at his sergeant.

'I'm going after Casey, Sergeant,' Forbes shouted. 'You charge those renegades.'

'But, Captain . . . ' Casey gasped.

Forbes turned his powerful horse. 'That's an order, Coogan!'

Coogan watched as the seasoned officer spurred his mount and peeled off the line of cavalrymen in pursuit of the outlaw. He cleared his throat.

'Bugler?' Coogan yelled out. 'Sound the charge!'

The canyon resounded with the haunting sound of the bugle. The cavalry charged.

There was no mistaking the sound of a troop of cavalrymen charging as their bugler heralded. For the first time since they had escaped from the reservation, the other Apaches ignored the words of Nazimo. They ran for their ponies and leapt on to them. They rode off into the desert.

Seeing his braves desert him, Nazimo defiantly returned his attention to the approaching sabres. There was no fear in him unlike those who were fleeing.

Nazimo spat at the sight and then turned back towards his prisoners with his rifle at hip height. But this time Hal Harper was not cradling the wounded Talka. This time he was coiled like a puma ready to strike.

No sooner had Nazimo's eyes focused upon him and the rest of the small band of kneeling men than Harper leapt up off the sand and caught the brave around the shoulders. As both men fell, the rifle fired into the sky and fell from Nazimo's grip. Harper landed on top of the Indian and smashed his clenched right fist into his jaw. The sound of cracking teeth came a split second before the Apache drew his knife from his belt. Harper grabbed the wrist of his opponent. They wrestled across the sand and rolled down into a gully.

Nazimo managed to rise first but Harper would not release his grip on the hand with the knife in it. They struggled like rutting deer. The Apache tried to take the knife into his other hand but Harper raised a boot and kicked out.

Nazimo flew back.

Faster than he had ever moved before, Harper got to his feet when he saw the blade glinting in the blazing sun. His hand went to his holster but the Colt had gone. The blade of the knife was like a mirror. It flashed in the eyes of the young drifter who moved backwards.

The furious Nazimo whooped and threw himself across the distance between them. He was only halfway to his target when an ear-splitting noise deafened the drifter. Nazimo's body was knocked sideways and hit the sand hard. Harper staggered and looked at the body. Then he saw the blood pumping from the bullet hole in the Apache's side.

He looked to the Indians and saw Talka with the gun in his shaking hand. Harper rushed to the side of the brave.

'I thought ya was dead, Talka.'

Talka returned the gun to its owner. 'You drop this, White Eyes Hal.'

Harper slid the six-shooter into its holster and then looked across the sand. He could see the raging battle between the cavalry and the last of Nazimo's followers. It did not last long.

'Them Apaches are done for, Talka,' Harper said.

Talka did not answer.

★   ★   ★

It was a lot further to the golden-coloured buttes than Talbot had figured. His mount

199

was flagging beneath him as he steered it between the cactus and brush in an attempt to reach a place where he thought that he might find salvation.

Then a shot came from the barrel of Eli Forbes's service revolver. The bullet hit the horse in the top of its muscular left leg. The animal crashed into the ground heavily and threw its rider a dozen or more feet over its head. Talbot came to a halt beside the base of a Joshua tree. For a few seconds he lay winded, then he saw the horseman approaching him through the thicket of tall cactus.

Instinctively Talbot's hands went to his guns as he scrambled to his feet. He pulled them both from their holsters and cocked their hammers.

For the first time in his entire life the man who had been born Robert Casey was afraid. One stiff-backed cavalry officer riding towards him with a smoking gun in his gloved hand was actually frightening him.

Talbot raised both guns and fired.

Red-hot flashes erupted from the gun barrels.

Forbes continued to approach through the gunsmoke.

Again the outlaw fired. Still the cavalryman rode closer.

Talbot ran forward and cocked his hammers again.

Captain Eli Forbes stopped his horse and blasted one more shot at the outlaw. The accurately placed shot went straight into Talbot's chest.

Talbot crumpled and fell on to one knee. The gun in his left hand fell to the sand. Blood soon encircled the kneeling man as he gasped and tried to raise the gun again.

Forbes dismounted and strode toward the outlaw.

'Look at me!' Forbes commanded.

Talbot coughed. Blood gushed from his mouth and poured down over the shirt with the tin star pinned to it. His eyes looked upward.

'Stinking Yankee!' the outlaw mumbled.

Forbes raised his weapon and cocked

its hammer. He aimed at the head of the man he had sought for so many years.

Then Talbot fell on to his face.

Captain Forbes closed his eyes and then returned his gun to its buttoned-down holster. He sighed and walked back to his powerful horse. He mounted and turned its noble head and tapped his spurs.

Finale

An exhausted Hal Harper sat on the sand beside the burly Coogan as the sun started to go down. He watched silently as the army surgeon worked on Talka beside the campfire. Captain Forbes had returned hours earlier and also remained silent. Eventually the veteran cavalry officer moved to the young drifter and his loyal sergeant.

'Will Talka be OK, Captain?' Harper asked.

Forbes smiled. 'I'm informed that your friend will survive, Mr Harper!'

Harper nodded. 'That's good.'

'Who are these Indians, Mr Harper?' Forbes asked, looking at the small group of braves who sat close to where their leader was being operated upon. 'I do not seem to recognize their unusual clothing at all.'

Harper got to his feet. 'I don't know,

sir. They saved my bacon a couple of days back but they say that their tribe ain't got a name.'

'Highly unusual!' Forbes observed. 'I thought that I knew every single tribe in these parts but they're a total mystery!'

Coogan got to his feet and walked toward the campfire. 'I'll get ya some coffee, Captain.'

Forbes gave a salute. 'Thank you, Coogan. Bring Mr Harper one as well.'

'Yes, sir,' Coogan acknowledged.

Harper sighed and looked out at the desert to where the soldiers had fought with the last of the Apaches. He rubbed his neck and stared at the officer beside him. 'Were you chasing them Apaches, Captain?'

'Indeed,' Forbes replied. 'They escaped from a reservation at Fort Myers and killed a couple of families on their way here.'

'Settlers?'

'Yes.' Forbes gave a sigh. 'They killed women and children as well as a few men. Sixteen lives lost for nothing.'

The young drifter stared out at the dying remnants of the sun as it sank far beyond the distant mesas. The sky was stained with ripples of scarlet. He then noticed that Forbes was staring at him. He turned and looked at the veteran cavalryman.

'Anything wrong, Captain?'

'I had a son about your age, Mr Harper!' Forbes sighed again. 'You remind me of him. He had spirit like yourself.'

Coogan returned with two tin cups of black coffee and handed them to Forbes and Harper. He then went about his business.

Harper held the cup in his gloved hands and blew into the steam before taking a sip. The cavalry officer held his cup and stared at the braves again, then returned his gaze to Harper.

'What are you going to do now, Mr Harper?'

Harper smiled. 'I'm going to ride with those Indians back to their land, Captain.'

'Where is their land?'

'I don't know.' Harper shrugged. 'But they say that they live in a golden-coloured mountain higher than the eagle flies, sir. I'd like to see that place.'

Forbes raised his white eyebrows.

'Sounds pretty good, son.'

Harper nodded. 'If it's half as good as its people I'm sure it's mighty fine, Captain.'

'Indeed, my boy. Indeed!'

THE END

Other titles in the
Linford Western Library:

LANIGAN AND THE SHE-WOLF

Ronald Martin Wade

Silas Cutler hires Shawnee Lanigan to track down the bank robbers who abducted his eighteen-year-old daughter, Sara Beth. The ruthless 'La Loba' leads the all female gang. When he tracks the outlaws down, he's staggered to discover the real reason for the kidnapping ... Forced to report his failed rescue mission, he takes work supervising security for a mining operation. Lanigan unveils a plot and ultimately faces a vengeful mob — aware that they can't all make it out alive ...